DAUGHTERS OF THE HOUSE

Daughters
of the
House

Indrani Aikath-Gyaltsen

BALLANTINE BOOKS • NEW YORK

A One World Book
Published by Ballantine Books

Copyright © 1991 by Indrani Aikath-Gyaltsen

Library of Congress Cataloging-in-Publication Data

Aikath-Gyaltsen, Indrani. 1952–
    Daughters of the house / Indrani Aikath-Gyaltsen.
  —1st American ed.
      p. cm.
    ISBN 0-345-38073-8
    PR9499.3.A44D3 1993
    823–dc20   92-54392
                CIP

Manufactured in the United States of America

First American Edition: January 1993

10 9 8 7 6 5 4 3 2 1

For my parents

DAUGHTERS OF THE HOUSE

Chapter 1

Mala couldn't see them, I'm sure of that. And she's near-sighted besides. With her feet carefully planted at least a yard from the edge and her hands rubbing together, she wagged her head and screwed up her eyes in a tremendous effort to seem interested, murmuring in the way she always did, "Do you think so, Chchanda? Do you think so?"

I didn't think anything. I have eyes in my head and I saw them very well, both of them, down at the bottom of the pond that the Koel sluggishly makes, under the netting of the trap: a long tapering one lying perfectly still, its nose at the mouth of the trap, and a round one swimming franti-cally against the sides of the net, its silver scales gleaming. Uncle Katla, Aunt Rui, the latter big enough not to go down the gullet of the former but still considerably nervous of his proximity. As for the trap, I recognized it too by its size and the shape of its meshes: only Wagner himself had one like that and since his little grey dinghy came sculling around the river these holiday mornings, it would be just as well to act quickly if I wanted to eat a decent meal and spare him a fit of apoplexy.

"It's cold, isn't it, Chchanda? Isn't it cold?" cried Mala, seizing my hand that was already at the neck of my dress. It certainly wasn't too warm. The siris still had leaves and the wild yellow iris still burned brightly among the reeds only just touched with rust and barely stirring beneath the sudden gusts that were twisting all the leaves still on the deodars. But the sky, as always a month ahead of the earth in Chotanagpur, drowned out the sun in the thundering greys of its advancing season, missing its usual leaves, its usual birds. The river was too cold, neither running nor still, not yet smelling of mud, yet rising a little, foaming, and softly rocking the boat that was dragged halfway up the bank. Too cold to dive in, but what else was there to do? If we didn't want to miss our chance to play a trick on our old enemy Wagner, and at the same time to supplement Parvati's larder, which leaned a little too heavily on rice and brinjals, I would have to dive.

I pulled my dress over my head. It was a nondescript garment run up by the village tailor from an old Sears Roebuck catalogue. It was old enough to be authentically "British," which of course it was not. Free of my dress, I slipped off the brassiere that hadn't had the task of embracing much since it had been discarded as too shabby for my aunt and revived, although really too big for me. Shivering all over, I hesitated before removing my cotton panties—but to keep them on would make matters too complicated later on. They would hardly have time to dry before lunch. Behind us was only a walled garden and across the river only ditches and islets of this many-channelled branch of the Koel. All deserted as far as the eye could see, without a single goatherd, a single cow, a single dog.

"And your hair, Chchanda! Your hair!" protested my sister. Too bad. The panties were off now and I was in the river. Once you were in, the shock wasn't so bad, and, with a push against the bank, I sank beneath the surface, scissoring my legs like any frog. The spot was encumbered with arrowhead weeds and half-submerged water lilies. I had to come up for air before I reached the trap, and it was too heavy for me to move. The bank, seen from the river, seemed to have grown higher. By now Mala was sounding like a one-child chorus of misgiving: "Come up now, come up. It's raining!"—which struck me as such a ridiculous inducement that I burst out laughing. But it *was* raining; the air was full of drops and the Koel was starred with those little circles that I used to call "tear-children" to correspond to the "laugh-children"—those thousands of disco lights scattered under the trees in sunlight.

I was just about to go under again when Mala trembled and turned around. She fled, so I wasn't surprised to see Parvati coming towards me with those long strides that turned up the edges of her sari at every step, bristling with starch and indignation, umbrella held very high and straight. In seconds, she was at the riverbank. I saw her roll her stony eyes, point her thick index finger at my little pile of clothes, and, even with my ear at water-level, I could hear the splendid beginning of her abuse: "Marcus! In the water! In weather like this! If your aunt only knew. . . ." The rest couldn't reach the six feet of water I had put between us and I devoted myself to pushing the trap to a position I could handle from the bank. In for a penny, in for a pound. No sooner was my nose above water again than Parvati began to bawl, "And stark naked! As if she had no shame at eighteen!"

In passing, let me explain that Parvati's "Marcus" was an interjection of unspecified reference. My aunt interpreted it vaguely as something out of the Bible. I had smelled out the recollection of an almost-forgotten husband, and a detestable one at that, since his name, over half a century later, could still serve as a term of such reproach. Whatever it meant, Parvati's "Marcus" was always a bad sign and necessitated immediate pacification. With a swift hand, one accustomed to this task, I unhooked the trap and threw Uncle Katla and Aunt Rui in two silver arcs to land at Parvati's feet, cutting short her diatribe in a grumble of ill-concealed interest and greed. Her severity softened. Her eyelids fell modestly over her stone-washed eyes. "Be sure to put the trap back where you found it," she hissed. It was back already and Parvati wiped my back as I got into my clothes. She was still grumbling, on principle, for the sake of dignity, but she kept her eyes on the fish, thinking up ways in which to make them go a long way. The fish, barely gasping, died silently in the regal manner of all great hunters who have seen enough of death not to be outraged by their own. "Hurry up now," said Parvati. I was dressed in four movements, and, with Parvati carrying the fish close to her flat chest, we began to climb the slope to our house. She stopped before taking the final lap of her path, so cruel on her heart, and said inconsequently, "You have grown up, Chchanda. I would give you some hot milk with butter in it but there is so little of it." I didn't understand whether it was the milk that was scarce or the butter.

Mala made an appearance looking like a slim doe in her brown dress, identical to mine. "A letter from Aunt, a letter from Aunt for you, Parvati." "Give it here," snapped the addressee, seizing the letter, which the rain had already dappled with blue-black spots and which she managed to open with a hunched action of triangular dexterity, fish on chest, umbrella supported by chin and shoulder, letter in hand. It was held away, held close, away again until the right distance was achieved. Suddenly her brow contracted. For three weeks now we had waited for this letter from Ranchi where my aunt had gone—alone. The umbrella began to slip. By the second page, it had fallen like a toadstool on its stem. "God wouldn't let it come true!" she murmured. Parvati picked up the umbrella and proceeded into the outer court holding it before her like a shield.

Across the outer court and through into the inner court past the purdah-wall into the kitchen. She laid the fish down and, turning to us, said, "Your aunt has decided to get married. At this age! She is almost forty-five! Marcus!" We stood around. Until about twenty-five one had the chance to get married; after that, one reached an undefinable "state." With her teeth clamped, Parvati started to flame the fire. She had to relieve her feelings somehow and what else were we there for?

"Hand me the pan, Mala! And Chchanda, why don't you clean the fish! Did you ever dream of such nonsense, Marcus! Marrying herself at forty-five! And who is to care for you poor, homeless, motherless? He will have you out before six months, you watch. In her sleep he will murder her and before that he will beat her. Oh, that I am alive to see such a day!"

Parvati is a Roman Catholic of sufficient education. At times, however, some latent paganism erupts, which never impresses us like at present. I moved to the old stone sink. The long, thin knife Parvati used for cutting was on the bench. She picked it up and in one swift movement gutted the Rui, out of which fell a little perch.

Chapter 2

My name is Madhuchchanda. There is a Mukherjee to it but time, events, and short memories have effectively buried it in the mortar of the past. In any case I was born and grew up in my maternal grandfather's house, and both Mala and I are known as "Panditji's granddaughters." With some exceptions, I don't have much reason to complain about my natural endowments. I am rather strong, my head isn't entirely empty, and I can't remember ever having to use a thermometer or take care of an infection. A favorable diagnosis, you see, and to thank my stars properly I musn't ignore large eyes, straight black hair, small bones, good skin, but above all, my great appetite for life itself, the hunger that makes us gluttons for whatever happens to us, the passion for living that seizes every breath—so that you taste the air each time it enters your lungs afresh.

All this love for living, however, flourished in a remarkably old house. Not that it could have lived in any other. I cannot understand new houses with their hard angles, their

orderly gardens planted with trees that grow in the ground
alone, without memories at their roots. Our house, Panditji's House, was, is still ten kilometers from Netarhat,
between Icha and Hesadi. It has grown from the earth and
is an abode, a habitation, and a site. I was born there, so
were my mother and aunt and my grandmother too. One
of my forefathers set himself up there. He came armed with
a master's degree from Calcutta and started to teach in the
Roman Catholic mission school. The house was on church
ground then, acquired from the sale of public lands, and the
purchase tormented three generations of Panditjis until forgetfulness, custom, and the acquisition of an adequate income by farming allowed them to consider themselves
among the gentry of the district. And since, Panditji's
House—originally a simple oblong of sandstone and red clay
capped with tubular *khapra*, had changed a great deal.
"She's grown her wings," Nani used to say, pointing her
sad nose towards the little row of roofs that stretch out over
the side walls, giving the house the look of a hen with a
plucked neck (the chimney) protecting her chicks. There
was even a sort of a tail attached later, where the washing
tub had been installed in a brick lean-to at the rear. The
whole spreading edifice drew its consistency from its patina
under the bougainvillea creeper that never tired of assailing
the gutters and every monsoon embraced the walls in a
vicious net of veins.

The symbolism is appropriate but the house has long
since lost its other network, its maze of parish roads and

paths that branched out over twenty acres of land. The old acres, sold like so many others to tenant farmers, had shrunk until there remained only the grounds arranged in a little crescent at the river's edge: scarcely two acres in all, of which perhaps a quarter served as a kitchen garden, while the rest, all thickets and thornbrakes, was occasionally cut back to preserve a few tall deodars that plunged into the sky, swaying in the March winds like so many demented witches against a background of confused clouds, soiled a little from the smoke of the chimney. And nothing else, besides a gulmohur tree that had been struck by lightning, a rubber tree that oozed gum, and a garland of madhumalati overgrowing a little lawn where the crabgrass strangled the last crocus and the last rose tree reverted to a briar. The wilderness triumphed here, over all that man had done. It was even more so in the animal kingdom: a furtive cat, a few fowls that laid their eggs under the bushes, and every-where else fugitives, nomads, overhead and underground— the insects, the birds, even a squirrel making off with a precious vegetable, a mongoose crawling among the eggs and another mongoose among the hens.

And a man who comes to us. Over half a century now Panditji's House has been a house of women. Women whose weak or inconstant husbands could procreate, al-most incidentally, in passing, you might say, only daugh-ters. You could tell it was that kind of house everywhere—by the untended garden, by the rusty hinges, flaking paint—by the whole abandoned outside in contrast to the gleaming interior that smelled of beeswax and glimmered with brass on top of old *sanduks* that shone in front and rotted away behind, waiting for arms strong enough to move them.

I have known five of the women of this house, of whom three are left. I lost my grandmother early, the last of the Chakravortys but always known as the Panditjis after the occupation of the ancient forefather. Nani was a wife at twelve; at twenty-two the widow of a probation lawyer in the Ranchi district court. He had more than ample time to leave behind two daughters—my mother and my aunt, Madhulika. Nani wasn't to die for another twenty-five years of an unfortunately placed cancer that prevented her from sitting down. I remember her in the way you remember a photograph in brown and white. I never saw her in anything but brown and *tussore*. Clinging to her inheritance, her beads, to the memory of her husband, she lived standing up, dry, solemn, thin, and almost always falling back into her armchair under the photograph of a man graduating with some unspecified degree in his hands, with a face so cocky and flirtatious that it was impossible to find in his features the august face of anyone's grandfather. And although Nani looked right for her role, she didn't perform it any better. She was a professional widow. She didn't care for the house or anything in it. She left it all—cleaning, cooking, authority of any kind—to Parvati, a widow like herself, whose devotion and ability seemed less valuable than the inestimable recommendation of having known my grandfather. Nani came on the scene foremost and only in her capacity as chief mourner. We loved her; she was inattentively good to us, but her death, which was a deliverance for her, was one for us as well. Her presence had made us ashamed of our laughter and our games, and this displeasure manifested itself in the clicking of her knitting needles, her meaningful looks, or just her limp way of holding her head, that inclination of her neck to the left as if she was listening to her heart. I hoped fervently not to take after Nani at all and I still resent bitterly the memory of the exaggerated romanticism, that little click in the back of her throat, with which she would spread out her fingers and murmur delicately, "A lily hand, Madhuchchanda . . . you don't have it . . . your hands are the key-holding kind." Unwittingly, these were the most endearing words she ever said to me.

This grief that Nani had decided to bear along with her name and daughters must have stifled my mother. Excessive and uncalled for, it became rapidly unsupportable for her. On an occasion before she died, she admitted to me that she had got to the point of hating this father, that she actually doubted the value of love and faithfulness since they were able to force life to such a deadlock. The consequences of such a feeling were inevitable and she rushed into marriage to escape.

Chance certainly lost no time in showing its irony. Kiron Mukherjee, a thirty-one-year-old journalist of Calcutta, inherited some land in Ranchi division with a house on it. He decided to throw up journalism and become a writer. What more salubrious spot than that inherited from his uncle? On closer inspection the house proved uninhabitable, but it was close to his wife's house. While elaborate plans were made to renovate it, he moved into Panditji's House. My mother never forgave the betrayal. I was born, then came Mala. Both daughters became living reproaches, a source of constant quarrelling, each parent accusing the other of having concealed some secret genealogical flaw whereby only girls were reproduced.

Three years passed and my father disappeared. We waited but not impatiently. After a suitable time we framed him next to grandfather. But he returned when I was twelve and Mala eight. None of us were happy to see him and he was unhappy to see the house stripped of its best furniture and fruit tree, by which we had survived, along with the fancy pieces of embroidery that Parvati took in and a few "loans" from her. For Parvati was much richer than we— from the compensation that the state government's irrigation department had paid her for damming the river Roro, blasting its banks and flooding Parvati's small farm. I barely recognized this greying man with the hesitant arms. Mother and Parvati presented stony faces. The only cheerful aspect of this homecoming was that the house was by now denuded also of my grandmother. Very much had happened within a short time.

My aunt, Madhulika, persuaded my parents to row on the river, away from curious us and disapproving Parvati. It was late afternoon. Inefficient at everything, my father seems to have had as little luck with the boat. How my mother, literally born on the river, came to drown we never understood. I did not hear his story. Suffice it to say that Parvati would not allow him even to change his clothes. He was chased away forthwith and we never saw him again. My mother's body was washed up on Wagner's side of the river three days later.

Once Kiron Mukherjee sent me a box of dried dates. We ate the fruit and kept caterpillars in the box. They did become butterflies.

The matriarchy of Panditji's House was a universe of nuns, young and old. It was an oasis. Mala and I had no reason to envy the normal family lives of the few children we knew, nagged by tyrants with penises. Like all country girls we weren't in ignorance of what are called "the facts of life," and we considered men of about as much use as the tomcat, the buck rabbit, the rooster who laid no eggs, the bull who gave no milk. Episodic characters, all of them. Rather useless and rather disgusting. Parvati's face, during the recital of certain village scandals after marketing expeditions and deliveries of sewing, told me how right I was.

What else is there to tell? That more than anything else in the world we loved this lady of the "pretty-aunt-smells-so-good" cult, a woman both lovable and loving and so willing to wrap herself in us that we forgot she was a human and a woman. Love, you know, takes advantage as it can of its occasions, which are after all what they are. Love. Mala smacked her lips and looked dreamy over it.

Parvati's righteousness struck it as full of principles as if it were a pincushion, flaying us all with her reproaches. As for me, although I tried to be casual and independent, I took offense all the more easily. Nothing could have been more cramped than my sentimental geography: Province, Panditji's House. Capital, my aunt Madhulika. Sub-prefectures, Mala and Parvati. The rest was foreign territory, so much so that, once I had my school certificate, I couldn't bear to continue my studies. Our strained circumstances provided my excuse, and I actually felt incapable of living anywhere else, of living any other life but this one, divided among the river, embroidering silks, and the one place that I respected: my aunt's bedroom with its canary yellow silk bedcover, its dressing-table, and its old-fashioned desk where she did accounts, eking out rupee by rupee of our precarious livelihood.

Chapter 3

Around eleven o'clock the restlessness, then the cries, then the short flight of the mainas retreating from reed to reed, proclaimed her approach. Almost at once I recognized the familiar noises: the slight lapping sound that swelled in the rushes and sucked at the red mud on the bank, the splashing of the oars as they fell back into the water, the rustling of the Koel divided by the prow of a rowing-boat whose keel grated as it passed over some submerged branch. And at last, two elongated shadows gliding over the reeds, among those wounded reeds recently cut by the basket weavers. Two shadows I said and I was right. Parvati and Mala watching from the front gate couldn't see a thing. My instinct hadn't failed me when I decided to wait, the house clean, the dress for Mrs. Prabhakar's granddaughter finished, down by the peepul tree at the end of the backyard, from where you could see whatever water traffic might come towards you from the south. They had undoubtedly come from Thakur Sahib's house.

Since they had already announced their impending marriage to us—who were women, after all, and could do nothing about it—it was easy to guess that it was now their duty
to notify, as courageously as possible, the gentleman across
the river, the story-book father-in-law on vacation on his
estates. And he would be rather more difficult to handle. So,
Madhulika, escorted by her cavalier, returned by the Koel,
which thus betrayed me once again. Across the Koel from
us, its orchards and fields swollen with the opulence that
care and ability bring, lay Thakur Sahib's house, a replica of
Panditji's but in reverse. It was a household of men and of
plenty. Wagner and his son. I refer to Thakur Sahib as that
because of his loud voice. A member of the chamber of
commerce of Ranchi and a lawyer. Besides being a landlord
of course. And Pratap Singh, his son, a lawyer like him and
like him, too, counsel for the mines and quarries of the
district. "Him! Marcus! He defends coal and stones!" said
Parvati, and for months she cooked food over firewood in
retaliation.

Once upon a time, I believe, the legal dynasty of the
Thakur Singhs had been friendly with the tutorial dynasty
of the Panditjis and Chakravortys, but the connection died
out with my grandfather, the last Panditji. His death, hard
times, our reduced circumstances, and perhaps, too, a certain displacement in the generations, a change in the way
our families expressed themselves, had broken the continu-
ity. Anyway, Thakur Singh did not call on Nani as far as I

can recall and we should have been free of concern on their account.

But, as I said, the river betrayed us. Ordinarily, to walk dry-footed from Panditji's to Thakur Sahib's, you have to go the long way around, upstream to the village, across the bridge, and downstream again over the low culverts that play leap-frog over the drainage ditches—a considerable expedition in all, spreading over six miles the six hundred yards that, for a crow, divide our *khapra* roof from the concrete one of Thakur Sahib's. Unfortunately, what separates can also reconcile. Suffering from a sort of riparian atavism, Thakur Sahib folded away his black robes and replaced them with gum boots and abandoned the meanders of legal ritual for those of the river. You could see his grey, flat-bottomed boat everywhere, maneuvered, I must admit, with great skill. Of course the old man with his blue jowls, his large hairy belly, his loud voice, and his jersey wasn't dangerous. But his accomplice! His accomplice who for years had appeared to be insensitive to the joys of country and aquatic life—as a little girl I don't think I can remember seeing him more than two or three times on the river: a tall figure, so serious, so wan, armor-plated with all his degrees—his accomplice had suddenly, tardily, come to life out of his law books and invaded our banks. There he was in his swimming trunks, everything showing, churning up the river with his dives. There he was in khaki trousers and a jacket, swinging a new nickel-bright fly rod over the water, landing the spinner fifty yards away in one stylish flick of the wrist. "How elegant!" whispered my aunt, Madhulika, one summer evening. I still wasn't aware of what was going on but I resented seeing him encroaching on our territorial waters.

My indignation lost little time in changing its object. Madhulika's faraway look and her sudden interest in the roots of the peepul tree and the Koel's edge opened my eyes. And the insistence of the gentleman in question. Now he was actually landing, that son of Wagner, jumping on our rotten landing stage, offering trips downstream in his father's boat, lessons in casting—so generous with his good manners out there among the mosquitoes—and there was my aunt, declaring that "it was ridiculous to have stopped seeing those Thakur Singhs, they're actually charming!"

So charming that my ears rang with their praises and I began to follow Madhulika and Pratap everywhere so that she would have no chance to be alone with that charm. My hostility and my silence confronted them everywhere. Useless, of course. It is so easy to become secretive if you have to. By winter the boat had disappeared and so had the mosquitoes. So also had Madhulika. She was going to Ranchi, she said. Nothing ominous in that except that the son of Wagner had his offices there. Parvati grumbled incomprehensibly and old Thakur Singh diligently turned his back whenever he saw me, almost as if he were reproaching me for something.

There could be no doubt about it: They had their difficulties with old Wagner, who was said to be very rich and must have hoped for something better for his only son than an impoverished, elderly nobody who had two nieces to bring up and who was three years older in the bargain. Perhaps he had even refused altogether—that was my dearest hope.

In spite of the notices (Parvati had verified them at the Katchehri), I clung to that hope while the boat, halfway across the Koel already, moved towards me against the dazzling sky. Madhulika sat in the stern and Pratap Singh, his back to me, rowed her towards our landing stage; but those sudden gusts of wind that kept ruffling the water and that carried the slightest sound so far, did not bring the slightest sound of words to me. Was their silence a good omen, a confession of failure? Or didn't they need to say anything when they were staring at each other like this? I choked back my rage, calling on heaven or hell to work some miracle that would hurl the dandy into the water with his degrees and his finery, so that I could drag him across by the scruff of his neck all muddy and ashamed. But while I instinctively hid behind the peepul tree, the boat came on, not even listing, straight on its course. I wasn't even to see him bump into the landing! The creature managed to ship the left oar just before he hit, and turned the boat on his right, so that it glided against the dock as if it were lined with silk. Already on shore, the son of Wagner drew the bow in and Madhulika stepped out, on tiptoe, careful not to catch her heels in the cracks between the floorboards. "Darling, give me your hand!"

And with that "darling" my anger burst out again. He gave her one hand, then two, holding the rope with his foot. Madhulika jumped out, exaggerating her delightful clumsiness, and stood next to him, motionless, watching him tie the painter around a root. She was . . . she was beauty herself at that moment, rising from the water like an Arabian queen in a fable stepping out of her mirror. And she paraded her abundance, the fragile insolence of her breasts, her neck, her eyelids, her coloring—that pale endangered bloom that made her cheeks all the brighter. And she said "Pratap" and Pratap leapt up, his hands before him, and there they are before my eyes, entwined, coiled around each other, heads together for a good long clinch—the fade-out at the end of a bad film. And I found myself counting seconds, one, two, three, four, devouring them with my eyes, five, six, looking for a flaw, the shame of it, seven, eight, because there's always something badly fastened, hanging loose, ill-balanced, in the statuary of kisses. But that kiss, warming my aunt like wax under this stranger's seal, that kiss had something perfect, may God damn him, about its movement, something irresistibly successful, something that let her soften in his arms and hang there without seeming ridiculous, even to me, nine, ten, something that announced my unconditional defeat.

When I could bear no more I leapt up and ran towards

Panditji's House, which was not more faithful than my aunt had been. For he began to climb the slope too, the interloper, with his new Penelope. It was imperative that I be in the house first. He would walk in like a new owner, fling his things on the table, take a glance at my aunt's room, at mine, and smilingly inspect this feminine kingdom of scanty linen, petticoats to be darned, of dust cloths made out of old sheets. He would sink into Nani's chair that no one had sat in since she died; he would take out his pack of cigarettes and the whole room would suddenly have a man's smell of cigarettes and sweat. I ran towards the house and even while running, thought, And won't it be splendid if it smells like that in here all the time, and our dear uncle beats us and makes us sit up at nights in the dim light to turn his cuffs and collars! What? Did I hear someone? Something? Behind me someone called "Chchanda!" And ahead of me "Madhuchchanda!"

I decide on the second. It is Paro, coming out of the kitchen with Mala at her heels. I am still panting when I reach her, but there is no need for words now. She understands at once, bristling all over, and crosses herself while the hairs on her chin become as sharp as cacti. "Your aunt's coming," she snaps at my sister. For all her acumen, Mala does not realize how the changed circumstances may affect her. She has already broken away, running towards the river, her round face wreathed in smiles, throat gurgling with affectionate cries. Just right. It would be too much to expect that Wagner II would not get a proper welcome from my idiot sister. Be surrounded by such affection! What a lovely future to look forward to, cosseted by our affection: the eternal gratitude of our semi-spinster aunt, a semi-Ruth rescued at last from her boredom and poverty; the pious devotion of a kindly old servant; and the almost filial assurances of my own tenderness as well—why, he'll be overcome! And to think he knows nothing of what's in store for him. . . . Paro, whose eyes have just met mine and found in them, as always, just what she was looking for, locks her hands behind her. "You know," she grumbles, "lovers and madmen are cousins. They don't think what they are doing any more than a donkey can say 'Our Father.' " She stands silent for a minute, pulls a sour face, and adds, "Of course, the likes of you would not understand it, but our priest said only last week, 'One sin leads to another.' Sometimes you can't get away without getting yourself in deeper yet!"

As far as Paro was concerned, deciding to marry as my aunt had done, so late in life, was a matter of sheer lust, justifying nothing. A new sense of Paro's conviction sharpened something in my smile. They would be living in sin and that pleased me. It whitewashed my vague cause, and blackened their own: they might have the law on their side but not public opinion. Well, that's as it should be. In spite of Madhulika's weakness for the man, she can never be his wife as completely as she is my aunt. It would be a sin for her to sleep with him.

And suddenly I feel how hateful I've been. But quick on that realization follows another horrible suspicion. Almost as if I had spoken my thoughts aloud, I bite my lips until blood comes, and, with a sudden gasp, I ask, "Paro, you don't really think . . . ?" Paro nods her head ominously. "Yes, I do. I have an idea your aunt is pregnant."

If she is, it's impossible to tell. There she is now at the end of the tumbledown garden, brilliant and slender in her cream and black sari. She lifts the pleats of it with one hand and with the other caresses Mala, who is capering with joy around her. I stand and stare, "on my life and everything around it." How could you do this? And there is no Pratap around. She must have made it clear that her return at least belongs to the girls. Delicacy has always been a point with her. My unhappiness is there for all to see. My knee moves involuntarily under my dress, my foot makes a step not easily checked. I realize Madhulika is worried—almost intimidated—by my guardedness as she comes forward. She makes a great fuss of putting away her sunglasses in her bag and removing a pebble from her shoe. Finally, only a few yards away, she abandons all pretence, "Madhuchchanda!" she cries, opening her arms wide. And what can I do? Except fling myself into them.

Chapter 4

Rains brought a chill to the Netarhat area. As a sal log split in Paro's fire, riddling the fire screen with sparks, Madhulika jumped in her chair and lifted her hand to her forehead once again. Silently and quickly we had eaten the fish, or what was left of it, as fish chops and soon after Madhulika had collapsed in her chair and groaned, "Another migraine! They've lasted more than a week!"

She had just taken two aspirins, one after the other, and the three of us sat around her now: knitting furiously and watching her closely. And a touch sceptically. Was she trying to gain time to avoid a scene? Around us was the familiar room. There were two sofas. One small, formal one reserved for the odd guest, usually Parvati's Roman Catholic priest who dropped in sometimes. The other had huge hollows in it and made a noise like a mutinous gang when sat in. It was difficult to rise from its sunken depths and still maintain dignity and poise. I never sat in it unless I forgot. Paro sat in a cretonne-covered Jeep seat. The Jeep had been bought by my father long ago, secondhand, and, of course, sold soon after. This was placed at a vantage point near the fireplace and from its disciplined non-depths Paro surveyed the room with an air of presiding over it. Beside it was an unsteady gate-legged table, steadied by two bricks and holding embroidery silks and a lamp with a singed pink satin shade. The singed side of the lamp was always kept to the wall, but had a furtive way of edging itself around the moment it detected the presence of Paro's priest, Father Monfrais.

On a shelf nearby I had a knitting bag with three separate unfinished sets of work, all of the same wool. In moments of optimism and elation, I would work on a sweater; in moments of reverie, upon a scarf; and to keep my mind off pressing worries, a sock. Occasionally, I would unravel the sweater to finish the sock. But more often I unravelled the sock to finish the sock. It all worked out to the same thing in the end.

Over the fireplace was a reproduction of Raphael's *Madonna in the Chair,* giving the room a kind of religious bravado. On the mantelpiece were unanswered correspondence, bills, religious pamphlets, two plaster-of-Paris Venus de Milos offendedly turning their backs to each other, a calendar. There were two bookcases on each side of the fireplace: the books you could see from the sofa were novels and classics, those hidden by the gate-leg and Jeep seat were old telephone directories put there for their bulk.

Between the windows stood a china cabinet that wobbled neurotically when anyone went near it or when there was a breeze, and it was cram-full of leftovers from services of tea and dinner. Presiding over these pieces was an open-minded shepherdess being mischiefed by a purposeful but legless shepherd. Along the tops of the bookcases was a jumble of family photographs; the ones without frames were tucked into the corners of the ones with frames, obliterating them. The wall above the bookcase had a damp patch, shaped like Iran.

Today was sock knitting day. Madhulika watched us and from moment to moment seemed on the point of saying something, then turned her eyes away and waited like the rest of us. Outside, the sky, flooding in the west, darkened until it looked like night. A warm, grey light filtered through the net curtains enveloping the furniture and the four of us.

"I've made the deliveries to the Ursuline convent shop for the linen and finished the uniforms for Father's orphanage," Paro said.

"Good," said Madhulika. "Get rid of everything you have in the house, and don't take in any more. Thank God we don't need to do all that anymore." Out of the blue smoke of the logs, oozing with resin, ran a flame thicker and brighter than the rest, a flame that shifted all the shadows in the room, retouching the three faces before me: Madhulika's suddenly not so smooth, and showing her powder; Mala's, serene but all tangled with snarls of her hair; and Paro's half-bone, half-skin, jaw and cheekbone wrapped in the generous fabric of her wrinkles. All three of us were strained, even Mala in her serenity. "Thank God," my aunt had said, thinking of the long sessions of sewing that Pratap Singh's fees would soon make unnecessary, and in her voice was a tone of relief that soothed me as well. If only the fees accounted for her decision! A rival can always forgive interest more easily than love.

Madhulika's implication served to start the discussion again. "Think it over, Madhu! Do you know where you're heading the children?" Madhu made a weary gesture that ended all debate. She hated the pet-name that Paro had cut from our common name to avoid confusion, bestowing the "Chchanda" half on me. "A marriage certificate doesn't make a marriage and in a small place like this people will forgive you. . . ." continued Paro.

"People will forgive me what?" demanded Madhulika, suddenly lifting up a face that was heavy with obstinacy.

"You know very well. Coventry. Closed doors. No friends for the girls and no good matches either."

"The girls have no friends anyway. As for good matches, Pratap's money will bring back any that my actions have driven away!"

My needles froze in my hands. It was cruel what she said but Madhulika had saved herself by her sincerity.

"You don't know what you are doing! You don't know," cried Parvati. "I've stayed here, oh so many years, I've brought you up and your sister, the mother of these poor girls. I've worked myself to death to hear you tell me you don't care what I say, what I think, what I do! So I'd better go to the kitchen where I belong. My dust-rags are cleaner than your sheets," she ended slyly.

But Madhulika had turned around in her chair and seized Paro by the hand just as she was rushing out. With her other hand she clutched my skirt. She had gone white. Her face, which seemed made for sighs, glances, soft smiles, was disfigured by an anger that tore her voice into harsh screams, Madhulika, whose words were always like pearls on a thread: "It's your fault, you know it. You have confined the world. I want to be happy. You want to have me here for the rest of all our lives. That's the way you love me. But I'm tired of carrying all the burden. I want to be happy. You are too demanding."

She hesitated, knowing us so well and afraid of hurting us. I thought, She calls us demanding because she does not want to give us what we ask. The economic necessity for Pratap had left me undismayed. It was hardly flattering to him.

"Try to understand," Madhulika continued calmly and with a pleading note in her voice, "I am not twenty anymore. After all, I'm a woman and have the same right to marriage and . . ." No matter how rigid she is, there is nothing in the world that can keep a peasant woman from the cradle and Paro's face had already softened. I was losing ground. I had to act fast.

"But aren't you happy with us then?" And my voice had the harshness of the very young. Madhulika's tirade had to be unsuccessful. I was not going to let it achieve the results

she had counted on—the tears, the hugging, the consola-
tions. We remained where we were—frozen, unyielding,
and hopeful. Except for Mala. On her face was the pleasure
of the giver.

"Pratap is in Ranchi," said Madhulika. "He will be here
to dinner." She was weary.

"The last bus has already come," said Paro, forgetting her
anger to this familiar, essential detail.

"He has his car." And then, in the curious silence that the
mention of an unfamiliar object like a car had earned, "Oh,
Paro, you'll have to move out the onions and potatoes from
the shed to make room for the car."

And then, hands at her temple, my aunt took refuge again
in her migraine, not insisting, not even asking that we make
room for the driver, as well, in our hearts. "A love like ours,"
I used the tired refrain intentionally. Once you start singing it,
you can't get it out of your head. Madhulika was angry at me
for my resistance but she was angry with herself as well for
her compromises and for justifying her actions.

"Come, girls," said Paro, very dryly. "Help me clear out
the shed."

I roused myself. It was almost dark now. Madhulika
went slowly upstairs. Everything I had stored up for the day
when the danger would be upon us—supplications, tears,
the Thakur's wrath—was of no use anymore. We would
have to yield to the invader, we would be occupied. But we
would defend ourselves even in defeat. We would never be
graceful.

Chapter 5

At first, I must admit, the bridegroom had luck on his side. Without having to ask her, I knew that Parvati, like myself, was lying in wait for his arrival—it was to be the first serve of a match—and I wondered how he would manage it, what kind of mask he would wear: the prince consort suddenly seated on the throne of an alien realm? But even if *I* considered his position and presence unavoidable, it was incomprehensible that Pratap had brought *himself* to accept the terms of a marriage that would certainly make his entrance into our lives uneasy to say the least. I reached a consoling conclusion at the last, even after the scene I had witnessed at the river, which was, after all, the most conventional sort of leave-taking between a husband and wife: They didn't really want to get married at all. And then suddenly, madly, they decided to do it at the last moment, and Pratap will be as ashamed of himself when he gets here as Madhulika was this afternoon.

But Pratap was to be spared the danger of taking a

position. By six o'clock, after four more aspirins, my aunt was ready to beat her head against the wall. She looked awful. Paro thrust a thermometer under her tongue: 104°. "Get to bed," she ordered.

Hysterical, or pretending to be, at having to leave us the responsibility of welcoming Pratap Singh to her own house, Madhulika struggled for the right to an armchair at least. But almost at once, shaking with chills and pain and, perhaps, not too sorry to escape the inevitable awkwardness, she let herself be persuaded into her bed, under a blanket.

And by seven o'clock, when we heard the horn sounding at the last three turns of the road and echoing over the river, there was no need to worry about thinking up a suitable expression for our faces. Once he was in the door any formal introductions would be superfluous. Madhulika's fever had melted the ice or spared us the trouble of breaking it. As I ran out of the house, I remember thinking to myself, as a matter of principle: Suppose I were to open the door and say, "Were you looking for someone? Mrs. Singh? No, you have the wrong address. This is the Misses . . ." But this sort of stratagem would have to be held in reserve. I ran out to the dark blue Ambassador as it was pulling into the drive, hurled myself at the rear door just as it was stopping, and shouted to the chauffeur, "Drive back to the village at once! We have to get Doctor Bose. My aunt is ill." The niceties were to be utterly disregarded.

"What? What's the matter with her?" cried the dim shadow at the wheel. His voice seemed to me too calm entirely. The car speeded up as soon as I had spoken and I thought complacently, So that's the kind of marriage it is! He could have gone up to see her at least or bombarded me with anxious questions. . . .

"By the way," I continued, "you probably know who I am, so . . ."

"You're Madhuchchanda."

I didn't answer. Who else could I be? The head in front of me wavered a little with the movement of the car as we passed trees, hedges, boulders, and fields transformed by the glare of the car lights into obscurity. We entered the village where Dr. Bose lived and then, "It's this house, isn't it?" I got out of the car the way I had entered it, without asking his permission or wasting words and without waiting for him.

Dr. Bose was out on a call. Fat Mrs. Bose answered the door and looked straight over me to the car. I requested that the doctor call at our place as soon as he returned and in those simple sentences managed to imply a wealth of suffering. Mrs. Bose would disapprove of lust veering its ugly head at the age of forty-five even more than I did. Or Paro.

Once again I returned to the car silently. Pratap had turned it around and lighted a cigarette, whose tiny red flame cast shadows on his features, tense with anxiety. He said nothing on the homeward journey. It was not until he had parked the car carefully in the shed, closed the doors, wiped his feet, and walked into the front hall that he finally said, with all the diffidence of a guest, not even putting down his suitcase, "Your aunt is upstairs, isn't she? Would you please take me up to her?"

The idea that this husband had asked me, *me*, to show him to his wife, as a traveller asks the lift-boy the way to his room, left me breathless with rage. If there was humility behind his request, I failed to see it. I looked up and for the first time saw what Pratap Singh looked like: a tall man, rather serious, even solemn, taking pains to look as if he were sure of everything, like most bachelors of forty-three. And with something more, or rather something less: too big a pocket handkerchief, a way of leaning forward from the waist, a fresh complexion spreading up over his cheekbones and slightly darkened under his chin by a day's growth of beard. I noticed that he was observing me at the same time and I could have sworn he was startled to find whatever it was he did. A teenage girl who scampers off into the garden showing bare legs and hair blown in the wind is one thing but the daughter of the house who received you in high heels and her aunt's sari and looks you in the eye to wit— that's something else again, and a good deal less reassuring. Poor neighbor, that was the least of your worries!

As I stood aside ever so politely to let my new uncle pick up his suitcase and pass, Mala emerged from the kitchen regions. Shyness fought gladness in her face as she went up to him. "I'm glad you're to stay with us, Mr. Singh. You're not Bengali but may we call you Pratap Da?"

Speak for yourself, you Judas, I thought, and with noble effort I said: "I'll take you upstairs."

And then, just as he picked up his suitcase, which he had set down on seeing Mala, the front door opened again and a kind of grizzly bear bustled in, saluted us roughly with his paw, and without further ado began to climb the stairs. "I'm in a hurry," growled our agreeable Dr. Bose. "Another delivery at seven. What's the matter with your aunt?"

"Chchanda," murmured Pratap Singh, showing further courage, still carrying the suitcase that made him look more like a stranger than ever, as if he had no business whatever meddling in the intimacies of our household, "Chchanda says she has fever."

Dr. Bose paid no attention. He wheezed as he climbed the steps and cursed them for being too high and of wood, dished in the center. When he reached the landing, he stamped his feet and cried out "Well! Well!" according to an inflexible ritual intended, he said, to prepare his female patients for his arrival. We had all followed him and suddenly our presence must have seemed excessive. "This is not a students' demonstration!" he shouted, as he entered my aunt's room.

I grabbed Mala, who had walked forward. Somewhat ruffled, Pratap stood, hesitant. I could hear Madhulika's voice inside murmuring something and then Paro's without enthusiasm saying, "Yes, what else?" and then Dr. Bose speaking into the wings, "Your husband? Didn't know there was one but if you are sure . . ."

And then, I'm not sure, but I think I remember pushing him from behind, that husband. He went in, still holding the suitcase, to be met by a little cry of pleasure and embarrassment and by two dry, cold, formal greetings. Dr. Bose would not forgive him easily for disturbing the equanimity of a household that he had always known. And Paro was there as well. She would do her part in our common undertaking.

She did it with the hand of a master. After ten minutes the door opened and out of it, in order of their importance, passed Dr. Bose, Parvati, and Pratap Singh. Dr. Bose's brow was furrowed, Parvati had her arms crossed across her chest, much like a man, and Pratap, minus his suitcase, but hardly like the man of the house.

Once downstairs, the doctor went into the dining room, where he always wrote his prescriptions. He turned to Parvati and said, "She's hatching something up there. I can't tell. Fever, headache, dizziness—that could be anything, anything at all." That was how he always talked, refusing to impress his clients with exact, complicated diagnoses and technical terms; it was a disappointment for his rural patients who preferred their money's worth of long words. He got out his pen and pad and began to write out a prescription in the most unprofessional handwriting imaginable, every letter and number formed as carefully as a schoolteacher's. Suddenly, he lifted his head. "As for the other matter, it is extremely unlikely and could be wishful thinking on your part and hers. . . ."

"You don't think so!" gasped Parvati, a sudden hoarseness in her tone. She seemed overwhelmed. Pratap had exclaimed something at the same time but was ignored by both the doctor and Paro.

"We'll know soon enough. I'll be back on Monday. Don't forget to save me a little bottle of what I asked you for. I'll need it for analysis. And give her broth with some of this mixed in it three times a day. It is only a sedative." He was ready to go and got up, all his joints creaking. He patted Mala's cheeks and said, "You eat too much," and took me by the wrist, "and you not enough." Then he was gone and we could hear his old car coughing down the incline. No one moved. Paro was in some deep thought, calculating on her fingers.

At last Pratap spoke in a firm, low voice, "I'm going back to Memsahib's room. Call me when dinner is ready, Parvati." Now he had really done it. But he was already climbing the stairs with the long strides of a man lost in thought while Paro looked as if she was about to discharge two pistols in the small of his back. It was a fine scene, one worthy to round off a day of such deceptions. Pratap had walked in only to learn that, perhaps, he, too, had been taken in, gulled like the rest of us by a magnificent pretense. By his very self-restraint he had botched his entrance, and then to make matters worse, he had committed the unpardonable sin of speaking to Parvati as if she were a servant. Didn't he know that for Parvati my aunt was "Madhulika"? And that she, herself, a naturalized member of the family for years and years, was only Parvati for us and people like Dr. Bose because our long intimacy had annihilated all the

hideous connotations of using her first name merely because she was our servant? I suppose Pratap called her
Parvati out of ignorance. But then, hadn't Madhulika
briefed him to call her Mrs. Horo until she permitted anything else? In that case, his mistake was no less serious—on
the contrary, that would mean my aunt had neglected to
define our roles in Panditji's House and that was adding
insult to injury. Pride bleeds faster but not as long as love.
It was enough to look at Paro to know she would not relent
for a long, long time.

"I'm going to make dinner," she said. I knew by the set
of her head and lips that she was preparing her counterattack. After intense activity with pots and pans and within
half an hour of Pratap's debacle she went to the foot of the
stairs and shouted: "Madhu, would you like some soup?"

There was a moment of silence and an inaudible exchange in my aunt's bedroom and then, "Just a little."

"Good," thundered Paro, "send Pratap down for it and
with him the clothes you travelled in and the shoes to be
polished!"

Chapter 6

The extent of our social life was the gatherings that took place after the Sunday services in the two churches of our village, the Lutheran and the Roman Catholic. The first had a rectory in which lived the Rev. Mr. Markham and his two beautiful elderly sisters, Eba and Elke. With their short cropped hair and clean limbs these ladies did any amount of good, never interfered, and the whole village was a little in awe of them. The Roman Catholic church was very entertaining, and whatever little formal and organized religion Mala and I had, came from here. There was very little to do in the village apart from these Sunday gatherings and besides we always accompanied Paro wherever she chose to go.

In pockets of rural India there are to be found these communities that are very Christian. Due to the beauty of the surroundings, a lot of retired Anglo-Indians have settled around, calling for a couple of churches, a convent, and the resultant conversion of the tribals. Finally have come along a few Hindu families—in the main, Bengalis looking for a cheap summer resort. They have built houses and then never moved back to the cities. The heads of such families are usually looked after by their daughters and when they die the daughters remain on in these houses, at times visited by brothers—from Calcutta. Insularity compels them to remain unwed and Miss Sen or Miss Chatterjee eventually dies, leaving all to a faithful servant or intestate, so that the brother comes along and sells the house to the missionaries for a song.

I think this was the fate that my aunt dreaded and therefore we had Pratap. I, on the other hand, could not conceive of a pleasanter life than Miss Sen's or Miss Chatterjee's, and therefore my hostility.

Early morning, Paro had taken Mala to service and it was Pratap who answered my knock on my aunt's door, a Pratap so wide awake and expectant that the door opened too immediately. *Et iterum ventures est cum gloria.* . . . I would have sworn he had not gone to bed at all, so as not to be surprised in his underwear. Hadn't he rehearsed in front of the mirror to get up in that bluff manner, that uncle-ly kiss, that hearty welcome? "Well, here's our Chchanda . . . Madhu is feeling much better this morning. . . ."

He would learn I was not his Chchanda, but only hers, on whom between my kisses I lavished all the pet-names in the world—my golden moon, my bit of silver, my white dove. My poor aunt was dumbfounded, but returned my kisses as fast as they came, grateful for the pardon she divined in this sudden affection, this exorcism by saliva. And in spite of my distaste for deception, I continued my little act for our witness until I had made sure he was well aware that, if the sugar was for my aunt, the vinegar was all for him.

My white dove, however, was an ugly yellow this morning and purplish under the eyes and complaining of lethargy. The bridegroom said consolingly, "It's only some sort of stomach complaint. Your aunt probably had trouble digesting the prawns we had at dinner."

"I think that's what it must have been," said Madhulika. "When migraine turns into a rash it always has something to do with digestion."

The words were Paro's but the prawns must have been Pratap Singh's and the allusion to some intimate wedding dinner made me flee in retreat to the kitchen, where I turned my tea into soup by dunking the bread into it. The hands of the clock seemed paralyzed and I waited sulkily for Paro to return to the house. The bells sounded over the fields and I plotted on making another ally, the awful gossip, old Father Monfrais. Hitherto, I had considered him to be too much of a cat to hold any position in the village but the time had come to turn disadvantage to advantage. Finally I left the house. Mr. and Mrs. Singh had not come downstairs and I was deprived the pleasure of refusing a lift to the village, which I had not been offered. . . .

"*Et vitan ve turi saeculli.*" Father Monfrais painfully hoisted himself up even as the last amen reverberated in the noses of the choir. Kneel down, be seated, kneel down, stand up . . . I obeyed mechanically but I was going to scream. Suddenly he turned round and started the *"itemissa est."* The last hymn sent the men into the street and left the women to their morning gossip in the church's square yard. Without hesitation I roughly pushed past Sister Jude, the organist, walked through the little gate, past the altar, and straight into the sacristy.

As a Hindu girl, little concerned with religion or social norms, all I wished to gain by roping Father Monfrais on my side was to have the Roman Catholic villagers disapprove of my aunt's marriage as much as I or Paro did.

The priest had already removed his chasuble and stole and his efforts to pull the alb off over his head now revealed, under the soutane that had been lifted with it, a garter-belt attached to a fine pair of black wool stockings. Having known me from my birth, he was as little enamored of me as I was of him. "What do you want?" he exclaimed, astonished at my presence.

I decided to spit it out. "I came to ask your advice. . . ."

"This is hardly the time," he growled, taking out his watch, "I haven't eaten yet. Well?" and then politely, "Is Mrs. Singh feeling better?"

Could I believe my ears? Not that it was surprising he should have heard of my aunt's marriage or her illness; in a village like ours everyone knows everything. But that a priest, whose faith and calling impelled him to bleed for the plight of two unhappy young orphans with a step-uncle forced upon them, should call my aunt Mrs. Singh, should submit to a name, which more than anyone else it was his duty to challenge. His little black eyes, their edges reddened by some sort of inflammation, watched me closely, their expression both inviting and pleasurably anticipatory.

"Of course, my child, this is a very difficult matter."

"That's what I mean, Father, I wanted to ask you what I should do, what attitude . . . ?"

Second surprise: "What attitude? There's no question of attitude. You are your aunt's niece and the daughter of the house and you will remain so!" He sat down on the nearest chair, a look of new severity on his face. "I understand your feelings very well, my child!"

Which was more than I could say. My own bitterness astounded me. What kind of sickness was this, disappointed in the anger of others for being less than its own, plotting ever-more vehement reprisals?

The priest would not raise his eyes, but shrugged his shoulders; his expression changed three or four times, knotting the intricate network of long, ill-shaven wrinkles that ran down his neck in wattles of dry skin. I could detect his embarrassment at having to invent new formulae for a girl whose faith was not his: the irritation of a clergyman whose parochial cares were numerous enough without being increased by trifling problems like mine—problems that were nonexistent if one let one day pass smoothly into the next, yet which seemed, nevertheless, to be flirting with them like the poppies with the wheat.

"Especially," he murmured, "you must not . . ." I must not what? He never said, but his hand stretched something in the air, pushed something away: misguided zeal, the inspiration that borrows the voice of angels to lead astray even the purest heart. And suddenly I understood myself. I turned away to look out of the window at the clusters of aparajita hanging on the window ledges, still wrapped in their cellophane cartridges. I was a hypocrite. I was using a man of conscience and religion to raise allies, forcing him, an old man, to contend against my enemy, enticing him to say, "Do everything in your power, child, to pull this union asunder."

But, alas Chchanda. No one said any such thing. The good priest quavered out his advice: patience, tolerance, and prayer. And more prayer. Besides sweet firmness in the daily accomplishment of duty, which is as precious in itself as it is an example. . . . And what exactly was it that I wanted? That was easy; I wanted status quo. The house, my aunt's love, living from day to day as I had always lived, Paro's care, Mala in the background. The old man was incapable of understanding that I loved each stone and leaf of Panditji's House and all of a sudden the entrance of a stranger threatened me.

I cried out suddenly, "But what can I call him? I cannot call him 'uncle,' and 'Mr. Singh' would be impossible every day."

"I think perhaps you can call him 'Pratap.' Really, Chchanda, don't clutter up your mind with details."

What was there to do now but leave the helpless old man to his lunch? Out in the square it was much worse. The drizzle of the morning had given way to a pale sunshine at variance with my mood. Irrelevantly I thought the colors of the world were several shades of yellow—like my aunt's bedroom. People still stood about the church lowering their eyes as I passed. They would burst into a thousand whispers as soon as my back was turned. Perversely, I longed for Pratap's car. He was after all responsible for my discomfort and the least he could do was to offer me the meager compensation of respect that all the village granted a shining, almost-new car.

"At your service, Chchanda, if it's any comfort to you!" Dividing the square, slowly pushing through the enemy ranks, the ambassador advanced. I wavered between the satisfaction of having my wish come true and the irritation of having to swallow my resentment.

And then, that imbecile of a new uncle had to make clear how much he had been thinking of me: "Climb in! I had to go to the pharmacist anyway."

Chapter 7

My memory of those two weeks at the end of September is not clear; the whole time is hard for me to recall without confusion or even embarrassment. Pratap lived with us like a criminal among his judges. Madhulika stayed in her room: her temperature had fallen but she still complained of sudden vague pains and uncontrollable spasms, and only her persistent rash kept me from suspecting she was shamming, giving us time to get used to each other downstairs. Dr. Bose paid two more visits—on each he was as distant towards Pratap as the first time and frowned while he considered the results of his analysis: "A little albumen, a few crystals—it wouldn't mean a thing if you were—if you were what you said you were. But now I'm certain the amenorrhea is only a symptom of something else. I wish I knew what!"

It was the first time he had ever used a technical word—almost modestly, as a casuist would slip into Latin. But at least we were sure of one thing now: There was no further question of a child, and Paro, still furious, hissed at me at least six times a day, "For nothing—she married him for nothing! My God, how stupid, how stupid!" The idea that Madhulika and Pratap might have married for other reasons never occurred to her, Paro's philosophy of passion being somewhat like her bun of hair: hard, heavy, and circular. "At twenty you fall in love and you have a happy marriage. But after that, girl, you 'make love,' you get caught by accident. I don't say it's impossible, sometimes it works out nicely, with the same ideas, the same interests—but you know that's not what's happening to your aunt. In any case it can't be love."

But what was it that made my aunt's eyes so brilliant every evening at the first sound of Pratap's horn? What was the cause of these sudden tremors, this haste to push away her book and dust her rash with an ineffectual powder-puff? And when Pratap walked into her room, what else could account for these exasperating little faces, little moues, these sudden drops in her voice, these efforts to snatch away her hands from my stubborn ones? And why did Pratap find it necessary to regard all these absurdities so uncritically, so affectionately? If he was disappointed, he managed to conceal his feelings very well and I can still hear his voice six feet from my ears, murmuring to Dr. Bose: "It's really too bad you know. We could have taken better care of her at my father's house. My wife could have got well faster. This house is primitive, the facilities are simply . . ."

But she wasn't getting well at all, and in the face of his

constant attention at her bedside it was all I could do to keep Pratap from making further inroads into our old intimacy. First impressions are often deceptive, particularly when they are produced by politeness or mere caution in feeling out the terrain. Pratap, without being exactly forward or even very skillful at setting people at their ease, nevertheless had the lawyer's knack of making just the impression he wanted, according to the kind of people he was with. It was his courtroom trick of throwing others off the scent especially when he considered himself baffled as well, that caused him to waver, employing several techniques at once. With informal clients his manner was "sympathetic," putting his visitor at his ease, identifying himself with the case, so that by the third answer he was saying "we." If kept at a distance, he became severity itself, reading your mind like a dossier in the pauses of a conversation. Then his slightly crooked smile would get the better of him and his solemnity and he became himself at last: a tall, serious man, with thick, black hair, whose voice, for all its grooming with care and his controlled gestures, trembled a little whenever his eyes happened to meet your own. It was this Pratap, of course, Pratap defended by his naturalness, Pratap retreating in order to save himself from disaster, who was the most dangerous of all.

That very first Sunday gave me an idea of Pratap's sudden moods, his startling candor. I sat in the backseat of his car, as silent and as ill at ease as a passenger in a taxi, while Pratap, smiling for all the world like a chauffeur who expects a big tip, drove me home from the chemist's.

Parvati was waiting for us, grumbling about the dinner, which she served at once. This time Pratap decided to stick it out downstairs and showed no surprise at being seated on Parvati's right. He bent his head politely enough while, to our surprise, Parvati recited the benediction, which she had never done before in all our lives. She crossed herself extravagantly to show how little Pratap belonged here. The mutton was saltless but he did not ask for the salt-cellar. As attentive as he was discreet. Our conversation however lagged a great deal behind our manners.

"May I have a *roti*, please?"

"Thank you, Mr. Singh. A little more mutton?"

Between monosyllables the silences were thunderous, and our paterfamilias, finding the atmosphere a little too numb for his taste, turned into the Man-of-Law: "Not very talkative, are we today?" he remarked, accenting the "we."

No answer. His hothouse smile froze but bloomed again, at the sound of the undercooked peas falling like buckshot from my spoon. Impassively Pratap bit those bullets and then, as if determined not only to smile at our mute desperation but also to overcome the silence with sociability, began to speak: a polite buzz that drowned out the noise of the flies against the wire gauze. The barometer, it seemed, had fallen well over a degree. There would very likely be showers in the afternoon, which would be good news for Thakur Sahib, his father.

"Thakur Sahib knows it always drizzles in the September afternoons," said Parvati.

"That is Netarhat weather," Pratap persisted doggedly. Madhulika would suffer, confined to bed. If there was a thundershower, she would feel particularly uncomfortable.

"Thunder," said Mala. "I am afraid, Parvati." Mala feared nothing in the elements. She dreaded unpleasantness.

But Parvati soon had her chance: "Madhulika is not a girl anymore, you know, Mr. Singh. And she's never been a healthy woman."

The smile disappeared, recovering again eagerly when I said, "Will you spend the afternoon here, *Meshomoshai*?"

Parvati was astonished, lifted an eyebrow, then dropped it, quickly enlightened: the man who marries a woman of middle age, a sister of the mother of her charges, is himself middle-aged by implication. If "Mr. Singh" was a way of avoiding approach to an outsider, *"Meshomoshai"* ridiculed him further with its suggestions of high blood pressure and greying hair. Pratap's smile and soliloquy ceased altogether, to be replaced by a scowl while Parvati in her malicious glee forgot to say grace.

Then Pratap's counterattack began. His eyes cold, his voice grave and deliberate, he turned to Parvati: "If you will permit me, Mrs. Marcus, I should like to speak to you about a matter of some delicacy. I discussed the matter with Mrs. Singh last night, and she is in entire agreement with my decision. For several years, you have been so generous as to

offer your services in this household without any remunera-
tion whatsoever. Now that Mrs. Singh has greater means
at her disposal, she feels, with me, that it would be unfair
of her, merely on the pretext that you regard yourself as
one of the family, not to recognize your devotion more
tangibly. . . ."

Parvati quivered and her starched sari sighed. How to
parry a thrust so veiled in agreeable formulae? "I don't
want anything . . . I've never wanted anything . . . !" she
stammered, piling dishes and moving towards the kitchen.

Pratap was cruel enough to follow her. "But I insist," he
persisted. "We'll work out a figure." He walked back to the
dining room, a man sure of himself, and found me shelter-
ing behind the sweater-without-end I always knit. In my
nervousness I had dropped one of my needles. "Porcupine,"
he said, "you are slowly losing your quills." Or was it
spine? After all, what had our little scene been but the reflex
of a man whose nerves were too much on edge—the spitting
of a tomcat that had shown its claws, but is afraid to use
them. An hour later he was curled up in an armchair in the
sitting-room, purring with good humor.

His warning, however, had not been wasted, as I realized
during the following days. Parvati beat a prudent retreat
from her exposed position, avoiding all contact with the
enemy, and contented herself with brooding in her corner.
"That man would be perfectly able to throw me out!" she
admitted to me at the end of the week. In her indignant fear
she had forgotton that Pratap had called her "Mrs. Marcus"

in all innocence. She behaved scarcely better with Madhulika, who, she had decided, was helpless to defend her,
and confined herself to the chores of nursing. It was enough
to watch her violently stirring Dr. Bose's potions or kneading certain salves of her own concoction with all the force
of her powerful fingers to realize how torn she was between
crying out, "Does it hurt, my darling?" and snarling, "It's
Christ in Heaven punishing you for your sins!" She confined herself, however, to speaking only the first of these
phrases, swallowing the second in the way she swallowed
her resentment when she was with Pratap, remaining on
the defensive.

And since I could scarcely depend on Mala who had an
overdeveloped sense of justice, the initiative was left to me.
I had scarcely the weapons required for an offensive. Not
even the courage—sometimes of course there is a certain
excitement, almost an exaltation in being perpetually on
guard, always ready to show one's teeth when others
would have surrendered. But nothing is more difficult than
maintaining such hostilities without arms, and how could I
be more defenseless? To join battle against Pratap was to
contend with my aunt as well and I dared not aim at one
for fear of striking the other. Ten thousand Hamlets could
not have been more confused. Knowing the tragedy that
would take place in the yellow room as a consequence, I
could scarcely hope very seriously to force my aunt into any
expression of incompatibility. The most I could do was to
"open her eyes," as Paro called it. But open them to what

kind of truth? What reality could disabuse her of what was, after all, her happiness? How could I accomplish my purpose and still keep my motives pure? How, without the dreadful little labors of beak and claw so dear to the carrion crow? One does not disguise the brutal fact that women do strange things before the climacteric. No doubt whole volumes might be written on this basic mundane theme . . . dramatic . . . analytical . . . in the grand Victorian manner . . . perhaps with that sly smirk that sees rich, deep humor in the gullibility of our human nature. But for Paro and me, the warrant was written in one word: intrusion. Could we have bought Madhulika's happiness with our very blood, we would have done so, but to defile the sanctity of Panditji's House with Pratap's presence!

My constraint made failure inevitable. What could I do except for a frown here, a pout there, a few equivocal remarks—all the apparatus of a feverish hostility continuously smothering its own expression? And what was there to express after all? A pained look concealed with difficulty, as if you were making a supreme effort to put up with an intolerable situation; Paro's sudden and offensive piety projected by loudly recited *Hail Mary*s in a Brahmin household of no religious persuasion, in an attempt to provoke an outburst from a liberal conscience like Pratap's, exasperated by such bigotry yet sensitive enough to wince at the realization that his mere presence in the house offended. On every possible occasion, we sanctimoniously parroted political opinions as blank as the plaster of Panditji's House in an attempt to contradict the well-known bias of Thakur Sahib for a government as red as the ore that one of Pratap's forebears had once mined.

(This was an almost unconscious expression of the peculiar political prejudice of southern Bihar that causes the rich like Thakur Sahib to vote left, as if to excuse themselves for existing, and the poor to vote for the ruling party, as if to maintain their shabby honor.)

And always, at every opportunity, the petty nastiness that is the special means of persecution employed by the helpless: to cough as soon as he lit a cigarette; if he spoke of his work, to listen with an ill-concealed boredom that was deferential until the moment when we could chatter of some village gossip he knew nothing about; to act as though we were liberated every time he left the house, dancing in our footsteps, a look of painted glee on our faces as he prepared to go out; or else to fall silent in pretended terror, interrupting the most trivial conversation as soon as he walked into a room. Careful only to avoid him or to forget him altogether, to treat him as an accident, an episode, a sudden hailstorm when seedlings are planted.

Or at least to try. I could not make an accomplishment out of what was only a tentative program. When you are helpless against the very presence of someone you detest, that presence itself can establish him against you, give him the time and the occasion to put out roots. Pratap seemed to be more and more at home each day. He had his routine, his shelf in the bathroom cabinet, and called our shed "my

garage." He also doled out the housekeeping money carelessly, decided to put in another bathroom, made improve-
ments. These additions to Panditji's House were like manna
to the starved, yet, at the same time, I felt them to be a
sacrilege, the recognition of his right to exist in our house.
Worst of all was the unbroken, ever-rising wall of courtesy
with which Pratap countered all my attacks: a wall parallel
to my own and as thickly crowded with flowers as mine
was with spikes and broken bottles. Ignoring my attitude,
not even deigning to acknowledge my feeble brutalities
unless his prestige was hopelessly compromised, Pratap
made fewer and fewer blunders, more often than not
merely repeating my name with a kind of ironic sadness in
his voice—"Madhuchchanda!"

Intimidated by his manners, inhibited from any expression of genuine hostility, reduced to the very crumbs of
insolence—I was at bay. I can remember going down to the
Koel alone and furiously skimming flat stones across the
water. I can see myself prowling through the woods,
scratching my legs on the brambles he threatened to have
cleared out. I would sneak around the dark house at night,
feeling things with the tips of my fingers or the soles of my
feet, congratulating myself and thinking—he'd never be able
to do that! This was my house! But I choked with spite
when I remembered he slept in the yellow room, no doubt
spread out full length, pleased with his rights, being generous, being patient, playing a fine role, believing we would
all come around in the end.

Something was chilling the cockles of my heart: the thought of never possessing Panditji's House.

I decided to look up the meaning of the word "cockle," lighting a torch to do so. It meant "heart."

Chapter 8

According to the pot of geraniums standing on a cracked saucer on my windowsill, it was the sixteenth morning since I had begun planting half-burnt matches in their soil, one a night, before I went to sleep, obeying some nasty village superstition Parvati must have told me about. The spell was slow but it worked. My aunt got out of bed that morning. Pratap was away running errands for a miner in trouble with labor inspectors, and it was almost like our good old times together: no jacket, tie, or collar amongst us; no baritone spinning out solemn sentences that made the air smell of tobacco, but four shrill tongues clacking away at their gossip, somewhere between laughing and singing. What a relief at last to discuss recipes or laundry, both of which we could now afford, thanks ironically to Pratap, without fear of boring the intruder. Why, if we wished, we could even lift petticoats and air legs!

The sixteenth day and the best for a long time. True enough, at the bottom of the fresh laundry were some shirts

I had pressed myself, with as many wrinkles as my pretended ineptitude could manage, but the shirts were empty of their back now and our house this evening was quickly recovering all its familiar and abundant feminity. Mala smoothed out rags with her nimble fingers for Parvati to hook into rugs, I was hemming, and Madhulika, her hand unconsciously exploring her cheek where the pimples seemed to be drying up, stared at the work basket, sighed complacently, and said, "Thank God we needn't take in embroidery anymore!" It was insufferable that our soup had to be thickened with butter from Thakur Sahib's across the river to blight this perfect evening with such a reminder.

And half an hour passes, all our old intimacy strained, the savor gone. And suddenly Madhulika looks up, a finger holding her hair away from her ear, "Did you hear something?" There is nothing to hear. The minutes tick away and I warily watch the pain that slowly starts in Madhulika's eyes engulf her whole body. Suddenly she is holding her head in agony, her whole body is trembling and her teeth chattering. Parvati is holding her right wrist while I stand by helpless, and then there is the sound of a car door slammed. Pratap strides in and for once we are glad to see him.

Dr. Bose had to make another call to the house. Pratap had chased him from farm to farm and finally brought him to Panditji's House after nine o'clock that night. I stayed with Madhulika while her temperature rose steadily and a new rash broke out on her shoulders, her arms and hands, spreading on her face into a hideous bat-shaped patch that formed a kind of angry pustular mask. Her temples burning, her joints aching, my aunt complained of sudden pains in her stomach, her chest—pain everywhere. And Parvati, climbing up from the kitchen every few minutes, filled the house with her *Hail Mary*s and *Ave Maria*s and whispered suppositions.

"Pratap? Is that you?" asked my aunt in delirium and Parvati stomped away, grumbling, "Pratap . . . Pratap indeed. You work your knuckles to the bone for her and she asks if it is *Pratap*!" More Aves are followed by Hail Holy Queens and invocations to the various saints responsible for the world's well-being, in the midst of which Dr. Bose arrived with Pratap in tow.

He stepped over to the bed, leaned over my aunt, and from the sudden intensity of his expression and the care he took to make his features register as little emotion as possible, I could tell at once that he knew what it was; that he knew it was serious. The air thickened around me. Parvati and Pratap holding their breath moved forward noiselessly, stiff as the images that sway above the faithful in church processions and at *Ramnavamis*.

"Do you want a handtowel, Doctor?" asked Pratap.

Dr. Bose shook his head. "Well, my dear," he recited to distract his patient, "you could say that you are really blooming and budding today. But it is always better to have it come out like this. . . ." Meanwhile he took one of Madhulika's arms and rolled up the sleeve of her nightgown and, while pretending to take her racing pulse, closely examined the white-centered reddish spots that speckled the back of her hands and fingers. Then he scrutinized the mask of pimples on her face with the same deceptively negligent care that only a doctor's eye can master and with a single anodyne "Good," stood up again.

"I must look a sight," groaned Madhulika, struggling to sit up.

"Enough of that," cried Dr. Bose, and pushed her back on her pillow. "No one cares how you look now and there isn't time to cover all the mirrors."

The man was obviously stalling for time, terrified of being questioned too soon, and he had backed gradually towards the door, hastening to add, just as Pratap opened his mouth, "If you don't mind, just to set your minds at rest, I'll come back later to make a blood test. I haven't had anything to eat as yet today and it's after one now. My surgery begins at two, so if you will excuse me . . ."

Thank God Madhulika wasn't strong enough to see herself in the wardrobe mirror, and I had discreetly covered the triple-glass Pratap used for shaving. For us to see our belle in her present state was painful enough and it wasn't true, "nobody cared." All you had to do was to glance at Pratap, whose every attitude betrayed an effort not to show how affected he was by my aunt's face. Poor lover, faint husband, how easily his heart had failed him!

Without a second thought, I threw myself on my knees at the side of the bed, and hugged and kissed my aunt hard enough so that she could feel my heart through the scabs and the spots. The same thought—call it defiance of contrasts—sent Paro to the other side of the bed, where she seized Madhulika's hand in both hers, and began patting and kneading it possessively. "Paro! Chchanda!" protested my aunt, "I might be contagious!"

"Not at all!" exclaimed Dr. Bose emphatically, "nevertheless, I rarely prescribe a continuous dose of licking for my patients. My father used to say, 'Infusions are better than effusions,' but I wouldn't dream of interrupting this charming family scene. . . ."

"I'll go down with you," said Pratap, close on the doctor's heels.

I hesitated. Now that Pratap had a pretext, I could hardly follow. Nothing would upset our patient more than having all of us rush out to interrogate the doctor at once. Paro began to mutter something about her stew. "I'll see to it," I said in a fever of impatience, fear, and above all, a need to show Dr. Bose that I and only I had a right to care about Madhulika; I was her blood and no newlywed husband could suffer on her behalf as her own niece would do.

The doctor was sitting at the little table in the hall where his pad and pen were waiting for him. He spoke gravely in a half-whisper. He had not once been able to smile at Pratap. My uncle-in-law listened frozen where he stood. At my approach, Dr. Bose paused, treating me to that moment of silence that tells you something painful is going to be revealed. Unlike most of his co-professionals, who prefer like judges to make you wait until they can call in several more of their kind to condemn the client, Dr. Bose rarely consulted a specialist and never kept his patients' families waiting once he was sure of his diagnosis. He merely stuck to time-honored village rules and requirements.

"I was saying to Mr. Singh," he continued at last, "that there is no cause for despair. Such things can be treated very effectively nowadays."

"But what things?" I asked, speaking at the same time as Pratap.

Dr. Bose picked up his pen and scratched three lines on the pad before answering, "I am not mistaken. It is something rather rare. In my entire medical career I have seen only five cases and then usually in an incomplete form that makes an exact diagnosis difficult. It didn't even occur to me when I was here the other day. But now the rash on her face is more typified. . . ." Three more lines scratched on the pad provided another painful interval. "I would prefer to be mistaken, you know. . . ." And he proceeded to write out the rest of the prescription. The pen's deliberate scratching filled the little hall. My hitherto unfilled brassiere was suddenly too tight. I was breathing through cotton-wool and I could smell the sharp odor of the stew that was really burning now. Dr. Bose muttered, "It's all right," signed and folded the prescription, and stood up for the end of the speech. "It's serious and it has an ugly name that you must not permit to alarm you. Of all the varieties of skin tuberculosis, the lupus . . ."

"Lupus!" cried Pratap, horrified.

Paro coming downstairs in her turn, drawn by the smell of the burning stew, received the word full in the face and stood on the last step, her hand at her neck, struggling with some undefined pain. Dr. Bose vainly tried to explain the details: it wasn't as bad as it might be—not the dreadful kind that ate into the flesh until it looked like a rat's nest—this was the exanthematic lupus, a different kind altogether, having nothing in common with the other. Then embarrassed with his own assurance he admitted that, although Madhulika's lupus was less spectacular than the other kind, it was also, unfortunately, less effectively treated even by cortisone, which had recently been working miracles. I heard not a word of what he said except "miracles" and the connotation of the exceptional, the frankly impossible, made my head pound.

Abashed at the effect of his words, casting about for reassuring phrases, Dr. Bose turned to me. Did he mean to bestow his pity on the innocent distress of Madhulika's niece only to refuse it all the more obviously to the spurious husband, who less deserving of sympathy in the first place, had been punished only to the degree that he had sinned? For a moment I let this poisoned barb transfix me, accepting the plight of this man as the vengeance of a destiny that would bind him forever to a wife disfigured in the very hour of their union. And then my remorse overwhelmed me: it was my aunt who was the prime sufferer and Pratap after all was only chastised to the extent that he loved her—

chastised for what was best in himself. The barb worked deeper, searching out the darkest corners, until it burst through the vocal cords themselves. I screamed and screamed, "No . . . no . . . no . . . !" Pratap stood before me, pale, his eyes heavy with compassion. No sign of the guilt that my baser self had hoped to witness. I knew that I was abominable. The screams rose higher.

And as I gasped for breath, I heard Mala's voice as from another world. That usually mild and self-effacing voice rang with a new timbre. "Shut up," she said with deathly calm. "This house that Panditji built was not for histrionics. It is too flimsy. Just like your emotions." And they all moved towards me, Paro, Mala, and Pratap. But Pratap was closest and my hand reaching for support did not hesitate to clutch his arm.

Chapter 9

The next few days, Madhulika's fever fluctuated between sudden drops and equally sudden peaks. The mask of pustules scabbed over, then spread, each pimple aureoled with white, reddish, or pale purple spots. The rash spread to her chest. Then over her whole body, as she sank into a clammy stupor, broken only by low moans wrung from her by sudden and violent kidney pains.

This symptom disturbed Dr. Bose more than any other; it proved to him that his diagnosis was correct even as he waited for the results of the pathology tests to come in from Ranchi. Somehow his dreadful confidence was easier to bear than uncertainty would have been. The old serene ignorance was impossible now. Every house in our small village had some medical handbook or dictionary with details that inflamed the imagination worse than medieval tortures. We ran to the Markham sisters, Eba and Elke. Their German medical handbook, which we were of course unable to read, said under *Lupus*, . . . "which in its extreme forms is generally fatal." This terrified us. We had known nothing all our lives but rude, good health.

But now the fact overcame even fear: nothing could affect us further, nothing could reach our hearts but hope itself and the sense we all have of gaining strength when confronted with our acknowledged adversary. I didn't even frown when Dr. Bose took out his syringe, adding, "I am going to give her the first injection now. There's just enough time. . . ." Injections were for babies just as hospitals were for the dying.

I stopped believing in Dr. Bose's smiles. He used never to smile before.

Since the attack began, Paro and I had scarcely left Madhulika's bedside, motionless, watching, laying out endless games of patience on the canary yellow quilt. Or knitting vaguely, something or the other. The moment she groaned, or murmured a name—nine times out of ten it was Pratap's—we would lean over to catch her words. Mala, confined to the kitchen and downstairs, made the most of the absence of Paro's and my hostility to treat Pratap with love.

Pratap's own ritual did not change. The front door squeaked as only Pratap, who did not know the mechanics of Panditji's House, dared to make it squeak. The rotten lath on the stairs creaked as only Pratap, who didn't know you had to tread to the right on the sixth step, dared to make it creak. And then we would see him in the doorway, his hair parted precisely, his trousers creased, holding his briefcase. He would say, "How are you, darling?" in an even voice belied only by the slight tic in his upper lip; he would walk straight to the bed, glance first at the temperature chart and then, quickly and almost fearfully, at his wife's face before leaning over to touch her forehead, very high up, almost at the hairline. "Don't try to talk," he would say, "rest my dear," and he would straighten her pillow and pull up her quilt with a solicitude that might have been genuinely calm or self-disciplined, or else already resigned.

Then he would step back, suddenly see me, and murmur, "Good evening, Chchanda," and I would answer, "Good evening, Pratap," or "Uncle" if I was feeling perky enough to be malicious. Madhulika, trying to smile a little under her scabs, would include us both in her remote, satisfied look. Pratap would open his briefcase, look through some papers and make notes. And at last say, "Let us go down to eat, Chchanda."

And Chchanda would obediently get up, disgusted with the sweetness that had become as prescribed and inescapable as medicine, permeating the house with a smell of falsehood. Disgusting Chchanda most of all was the suspected readiness with which you breathed it in. No matter how provisional your truce might be, there was no avoiding the fact that you abided by its conditions without much discomfort—not relenting but not rebellious either; instead, betrayed by the secret slope down which an attitude slides, until it becomes a habit.

I had passed the torch to Paro now, and since I was no longer in the field, she threw caution to the winds. She multiplied her hostilities, her hints, her references, her asides, but not to much purpose. Pratap made it clear that he earned the bread and the jam too. Paro's "I am unused to such a large household" or "I am not used to looking after men" went unheeded by Pratap. All the same she scored one point in persuading Pratap not to sleep in the yellow room anymore. He seemed all too eager to comply and Paro was left with an empty victory. "A woman in her condition—and her requirements are not always pretty ones—would be embarrassed by any man, even her husband. And after all she isn't really used to you. Take my room, and I'll put in a cot here next to Madhu."

And Pratap deceptively agreed. I call it deceptive, but perhaps I could apply the word more appropriately to myself, since I can't find a better word to explain the vague uneasiness I began to feel. Just as I can't explain the reason Pratap agreed to Paro's proposal so easily—out of delicacy, probably out of cowardice too, or just to be able to sleep better during a time when his clients were making particularly heavy demands on his energy. Or all of these reasons at once: good or bad, aren't all motives interlocked with one another?

And I suspect they were no less confused under Paro's tight topknot; she was quite as capable of being tactful with Pratap when she found it to her advantage, as she was of profiting by the occasion with Madhulika, making it quite clear how easily the bridegroom's stomach was turned by her new and hideous looks. And still Paro was able to arrange matters with her patron saint by telling herself she was doing everything so as to be able to look after her charges. After all, the priest would like to hear that there was only so much you could do in a Brahmin household, with a Thakur interloper thrown in for good measure!

Chapter 10

It was the next day or the day after, I don't remember, that I noticed my geranium. Awakened by my alarm clock, I got up, went to the window and found it on the sill, withered by the dry cold that comes over the northern Chotanagpur plateau. I had forgotten it along with the matches of my calendar. I leaned over it, shrugging my shoulders. We were through with such child's play now. There was a more difficult game on our hands, against an antagonist more dangerous than Pratap. Even if Madhulika was better now—a few cortisone injections had literally raised her from the dead—how long would it last? And at what cost? Would we ever see her old face again? That lovely cameo profile, that raw wheat-colored skin?

As far as I could see, the countryside was hardened with cold, the Koel river paralyzed under a thin and lazy mist. My room was cold too, and I threw an old cardigan over my shoulders without bothering to put it on. It was my turn to go downstairs and open the windows and light the kitchen

range. My turn and I was glad. It was just the sort of thing
I liked, that shivering work in the cold dryness of the
morning, in the soundless shadows that hung about even
the most ordinary objects until the sudden movement of the
winter sun spattered them with light. No other time of the
day makes everything smell so sharply, makes your fingers
so sensitive to the feel of things, the individual texture of
their surfaces that rises almost like gooseflesh on your upper
arms. For me, Panditji's House, I think, will always be as it
was then, the-house-in-the-morning, when the air is rarer,
the walls and the trees gathered more concretely into themselves, as if shrunk within the compass of your hand and the
breadth of your gaze. It could be the blinding sunrise of a
May morning, the vociferous downpour of an August
dawn, or the stiffening cold of December.

It was a morning like one of these last, as I said, and I
hurried from window to window, turning the iron handles
and pushing open the shutters without a sound. In spite of
my efforts at silence, one of the kitchen windows banged
against the wall, scaring out a reddish tomcat who wiped
his face on the cold grass and, giving me a knowing backward look, vanished into the gloom towards Thakur Sahib's
house, as if with many tales to tell.

I turned my attention to the old stove and of course one
of the lids had to clatter (the middle one "A" natural). The
smallest one rang a questionable "B." The biggest one,
being cracked, didn't sound at all. Before long the kindling
was alive under a shovelful of coal and I went into the living

room to get an old copy of *The Statesman* to use as a brand. Soon I was crouching in front of the fire, which needed no assistance from *The Statesman*; I put the milk on to boil and was reading an editorial by Pran Chopra, who seemed to think someone or the other had become a cult-figure. I could afford to read, now that the fire was off to a good start.

My stomach was roasting but suddenly I felt a cold draft in the small of my back. Someone had opened the door. "What are you doing here? Roasting a goat?" The voice was a familiar one but its owner had no reason to be down so early, sneaking around in his slippers and, incongruously, a *tush* shawl thrown over his shoulders, probably belonging to his old father across the river. I pulled my sweater closer around me. His eyes had a look similar to the tomcat's but all he said was, "Can you tell me where Paro keeps her store of soap? I've run out of mine."

The soap! It seems ridiculous how important little details like that can become. And how difficult to know the precise moment when mere chance stops being chance in order to become an occasion, a pretext. To know the place where we yield to the slope, like a skier beginning to urge on his descent.

There was Pratap with a perfectly good excuse and there was I staring at this creature whose masculinity was so at odds in our ramshackle kitchen. It also occurred to me at that moment that he was used to a far better standard of living. Anyway, he looked suspect. The soap story was a little too good. I handed him a bar out of the "Closet-for-

Things-That-Smell" (so that the flour would not smell of Lux).

"I want to talk to you for a minute," he said.

So we were going to be formal. And serious. But there was an intimacy that thickened his voice and filled his mouth with saliva. I was repelled and at the same time hypnotized into stillness. "I am glad of this opportunity. First of all I want to thank you for the effort you've been making to accept my presence here. I know that you are not exactly mad about me. . . ."

He waited for some sort of protest which my silence refused. But his skin was thick enough, for he continued and became personal again. "But at least you seem to be able to stand my presence in this house. And now that your aunt is getting better, we can all relax a little from that worry. I'd like to make you a proposition. That four women have to run this house seems to me a bit extreme. Granted that one is an invalid at this moment, and Mala is little more than a child. Actually a child. If you were to get a job . . ."

"Oh no! I wouldn't leave Netarhat for anything."

"It's not a question of leaving. . . ."

Indeed! So he wanted me out? Or all of us out? So that Wagner could take over Panditji's place, the land he had always coveted. It had been a marriage of convenience after all, only I thought the convenience was on my aunt's side. It seemed more farsighted now. I knew Madhulika would not mind leaving the place. It had never held for her the meaning it embodied for me: It was the fifth member of our family, the open space marked by our four corners.

But here was Pratap insisting, "Try to see it my way, Chchanda. I need an assistant. I have too much work to handle alone and my juniors are overworked. In any case they are not secretaries. The nuns have taught you well enough to type and file a little. Now Mala is a different matter. She deserves a bigger world and it is not too late for her. She is intelligent and less clear-headed than you, which is an advantage. But to come back to you. I haven't the means or the intention of lining your nest with gold but I can give you a fair wage. Get some new clothes. . . ."

Clothes! Like in *Femina*! I started to think, my nose pointed to the floor, my mouth tight. What was at the back of his mind? Getting me used to town life, its pleasures, its facilities, giving me a taste for another kind of existence so that in the end it would be easier to wean me away from the soil of Panditji's House and hand over the untenanted package to Thakur Sahib? A fair wage? In matters of money, Pratap had reasonable, which is to say just sufficient, like all good reasoning.

"And I think it would be good for you, Chchanda," Pratap continued. "You are always at such a loose end here, and at the same time so confined. If you think this house and this village are the beginning and the end, it is all right with me. And there is something to be said for 'roots.' But even roots have to be exposed to light and air, as you do with roses in winter. Do you understand me? How can you know what you want out of life if you have never seen what the world has to offer? Start with a little cash, a lipstick or two, some eye-shadow, coffee with people of your own age. I don't know. Your aunt and Paro have not done the right thing by you. Maybe there were financial restraints. But, by God, it will be different for Mala. She was born to laugh, to learn to grow outwards."

What was I to say? "At a loose end" was flattering. And as for Mala, I knew every word he spoke of her was true, I knew goodness and beauty and worth when I saw it but no one had put it in so many words before. As for a world that spread so infinitely beyond our own, it hadn't tempted me before. It didn't exactly tempt me now and I couldn't understand why I felt as ready to accept as to refuse.

"Think it over some more," said Pratap, and flipping the soap from hand to hand, he went back upstairs.

Chapter 11

Don't just stand there, do something! Put more kindling
into the fire, take the milk off the stove, put the water on
to boil—my aunt drinks weak tea, Pratap has coffee. Paro,
Mala, and I have ours boiled with milk and sugar. They are
coming to life upstairs now; taps are running, toilets flush-
ing. Paro screams, "That Mala! Marcus! Did you ever hear
of such stupidity? Such meanness? Madhu asks for a mirror
and she brings her one! Chchanda, go upstairs, your aunt is
having hysterics!"

I rush upstairs, taking the stairs two at a time, and into
the yellow room where Madhu is lying flat, a hand mirror
on her stomach. She is not having hysterics. There is that
same mirror I used to try to pluck my eyebrows once, the
mirror whose career is becoming more and more desperate.
It would be better if my aunt were in tears; her tears have
always fallen and dried fast. But she merely turns towards
me, with a terrible slowness, her face—that face that two
months ago was for all of us our pride and our example,

which this morning seems even more ravaged and ruined by the knowledge of what it has become. . . . And Madhu does not even mention her looks now, only saying with a terrible vagueness, "Did Pratap talk to you about working for him?"

A nod, a kiss, are no help in drawing her from the abyss of meditation in which she is plunged—a moment more and I'll be in it too. Why did Pratap tell her of his plans without consulting me? He hasn't even been in the yellow room this morning. He must have talked to her last night. Couldn't I be given the dignity to make up my own mind? And now Madhu, emerging from her reverie, says, "Help him, Chchanda, he has so much on his mind. Be with him. I have not been of much use to him; rather the reverse. But for me, Thakur Sahib would not have broken with his only son." She stares at me out of her dark brown eyes, which are all that are left of her face except for the perfect line of her chin.

(All this seems a long time ago; today I am a mother, a babe is in my arms. I keep looking at the flowing Koel and think, Madhulika was the most beautiful woman I have ever seen.)

If that was what she wanted, it would be that way. At dinner that evening I glanced furtively at Pratap, startled to find only the same affable man entrenched behind his plate, carefully chewing his food while thinking up what he'd say in court the next day. Caution for caution, Pratap immediately looked away. When serious-minded men decide to give you time to make up your mind, there's only one thing you can do: Take as long as you like and let them rot in their own discretion.

But it wasn't to be. Paro, scrupulous about all household matters, said, "Chchanda, go through the trunks in the storeroom tomorrow and take out the old linen night-dresses. We will boil them—Madhu should wear only the softest things now."

And I answered back, "I don't think I'll have the time. I am going to Ranchi to work for Pratap from tomorrow on."

Paro sank back visibly while Pratap added, as if in compensation, "I will bring the softest and prettiest of night-dresses for Madhu; no old ones, please."

There could be no secrets about my expedition: ever since her own vague husband, Marcus, had vanished into its purlieus, ever since my aunt had brought back Pratap from its center, each venture into Ranchi gave rise to all sorts of palavers and injunctions. For Parvati, Ranchi was Babel and Babylon, Sodom and Gomorrah; a place of confusion and lewdness, above all of insecurity. Stupefied by my sudden decision, embittered and hurt, she started her counterattacks the next morning: "He's getting around all of you! Just like your aunt—whoever speaks last is the one you believe. . . ."

I was unshaken by her tirades. Only a little embarrassed, and concerned about keeping Paro from believing in a volte-face I couldn't admit to myself. I protested weakly: Why miss an opportunity that looked so promising? I would earn something. There was no transportation problem. What was the danger?

Paro only shook her head, eyes full of hurt and betrayed loyalty. "Your aunt, I know what she is after. She wants the world to think we have taken to him, his money, his car. That he is one of the family! The danger, my little fool"—it was the last argument left in her throat and she spat it out—"is if his friends in Ranchi have the same ideas, the same habits, that he had with your aunt, God save you!"

I walked out to Pratap's car without a backward glance, wearing one of my aunt's saris.

Of course Paro was exaggerating. The things that are obviously distortions produced by explosions of temper manage to disguise the things that are true as well, and Paro should have known this better than anyone else. One of her favorite sayings from the stock of proverbs she used against scandal-mongers was: "If you want to be a wolf and don't show your fangs, you are still only a sheep!" This wolf had no fangs as it happened, only two rows of splendid teeth that shone perhaps a little too complacently when he smiled. He seemed quite sure of what he was doing, as if the new professional character in which I was about to see him would impress me far more than the family man I knew.

He was not mistaken. Pratap maintained an office-cum-flat in one of the older buildings off Ranchi's snakelike main road. I had heard about its spick-and-spanness from my aunt. After a swift and careful drive down hilly ghat roads, we reached his first floor office at about nine A.M. It seemed to provide a perfect setting for Pratap, exactly the opposite of Panditji's House, where nothing could hint at what he was worth; in fact, where everything worked against him, ridiculed him, beginning with his very status as our compulsory guest. Over "his" threshold, the tables were turned and all the little tricks I had played on him at Netarhat, his strangeness in our surroundings, his ignorance of the simplest domestic arrangements, the actual xenophobia that a strange house always has, all turned against me. Not that Pratap was a stranger to Netarhat; his house was just a narrow river's span away—but it could be another country!

"Do you like it?" asked Pratap, entirely at ease.

Yes and no. I liked it well enough for him, not at all for me. Rooms are like clothes and what feels comfortable on one body is desperately tight on another. The most ordered interior, where space is so carefully distributed that you have to breathe in keeping to time, inhibits the forest nymph who yearns for her tender jumbles. These bare blue-grey walls, relieved only by the large curtained windows in stark black and white, shapes of furniture very clean, steel and glass in odd utilitarian shapes. All this was not compatible with my own tastes, my own crowd of old furniture, brass knickknacks, copper pots that shone like signals in the darkness of Panditji's House. I started to feel cold even though we had descended to a height of some fourteen hundred feet only. It happened to be the air conditioner in December, to "air" the place, Pratap said. The kitchen, so clean, so useless. I longed for Paro to see it. She would love to throw some potato peels around and hang up black-bottomed pots and pans. Only the bathroom with its marble tiles and recessed shower stall made my mouth water.

"And here is a small bedroom," said Pratap. I looked in through the doorway, my feet refusing to enter. Wasn't this the same carpeting over which Madhulika had walked, towards that bed? On the bedside table was something Paro had missed from our house about two years ago—a malachite Ganesh. I remembered Madhulika keeping very quiet about it.

Pratap was speaking: "You sit over there, in the office, at the little table. When I have a client—there are usually about ten or twelve a day—you will show him in here, and if I say, 'Thank you, Miss Mukherjee,' you will leave us alone. You will get the hang of it, I am sure."

"Did Madhu give you that Ganesh?" I asked.

"Yes, Miss *non sequitur*," he said.

He didn't have to say, "Thank you, Miss Mukherjee," or didn't dare to all morning long. I filed papers, each one in its own manila envelope mysteriously arranged according to occupation: agriculture, coal mining, hardware, and so forth. "The Joint Stock Company of Jain Minerals . . . no, under iron ore . . . no, that's the board of directors, I want their lawyer. Look under LLB. Find it?" And after noon I introduced my first clients, a pair of farmers who looked, I thought, quite unimportant, until Pratap asked them for funds and they counted out, one by one, not even frowning, one hundred rupee notes. I scarcely understood their conversation, crammed with figures and references to the revenue department, but I made myself busy transcribing an address or a date for an appointment whenever Pratap would turn around and say, "Make a note of that, please." His tone was a little forced, but try as I would to reawaken some of my old resentment by telling myself that his solemn manner fitted his face like a mask of kaolin, it was undeniable that Mr. Singh was an altogether different person from my aunt's husband. This was not my hoped-for petty lawyer, asking pettier magistrates for extensions of dates.

His new authority, his competence, even if I couldn't verify it, made their effect on me, inspired a new hesitant esteem, a certain fear even, and above all, a new kind of irritation: What a fool that girl back at Panditji's House seemed now, carrying on guerilla warfare, needling this man who was strong enough even to permit himself a certain affection for her, the weakness of opposing me and Paro with the light armor of sympathy and consideration. I had hoped to show contempt of counsel, or even better, try to conceal it thinly; and I could feel no contempt!

Which was why Pratap's quick, almost-furtive gesture of counting through the farmers' notes and locking them up in his drawer comforted me a little: That was the kind of fault I wanted him to have.

It was well past noon. "Will you come out to lunch with

me or go shopping or both?" he asked.

"Go shopping," I said at once. "By myself."

"Right," he said, taking out, I think, five of the farmers' notes. "An advance. I will pay fifteen hundred rupees a month. Now walk to the main road, turn right, and at the intersection is Dayarams. Be careful about traffic."

I knew Dayarams. We shopped there for linen, blankets, wool, a few clothes, whenever a meager fixed deposit of my aunt's matured. It was an excellent shop with excellent prices. I went up to the intersection and turned left into Refugee's Market instead. All the shops here were owned by Sikhs; all of them called you *bahenji*, and you could bargain like mad. I bought two salwar kurta sets, a blue for Mala and a saffron for myself; an orange lipstick; and a kohl pencil. Across the street, I went into a beauty parlor, had my hair cut, my eyebrows tweezed, and makeup put on me professionally. Outside the postgraduate building, I ate two samosas and washed them down with a glass of tea, feeling all the time as obscure as Jude. I dashed back to Pratap's office: he was out, thank God. I showered quickly without wetting my face and put on the new clothes. Out again and to hell with clients or phone calls; this time I went into a five-star hotel's flower-shop and blew one hundred and thirty rupees on a bonsai pot of bougainvillea for Paro.

It was late before Pratap returned. He looked at me. "Too pretty and too cheap." Can anything be too pretty and too cheap? He himself carried a large Dayarams box under his arm. "Let us go," he said, "this blasted drive is too long."

He seemed in a bad mood. I liked the shape of his hands on the steering wheel or just the fact that I had a car to sit in instead of the slow bus we hitherto used to take to Netarhat with our shopping parcels.

Chapter 12

I am a little confused with my story at this moment of time. I prefer to think of myself as a positive, logical sort of woman. I dislike remembering those troublesome backwaters, those black hopes that Pratap and my aunt would fall apart, aided by the efforts of Paro and myself and, of course, the terror of Thakur Sahib's prolonged disapproval of the whole unhealthy business. Those backwaters prevented my life from running its smooth, even course.

December, January, February. How can I forget them? The southeastern winds blew and blustered. I like the wind when he is showing off along the mud roads, blowing women's saris, taking the washing from the lines and generally playing merry hell. But in a winter mood and shape he is terrible, an animal in shadows, waiting to spring—and with claws. And the country he has been thrashing to death lies low, awaiting the next blow. That is the wind-silence. Terrible is this silence, this threat. It comes through cracks and crevices in old houses to sit with you, haggard and fearful, snatching at unuttered words, pressing cold fingers around hearts. You cannot see him but there he is in the lull, a scent of danger caught in the forest air. The stink of the festering teeth of a tiger that flies to the nostrils of the trapped hunter. And so the wind followed us to Netarhat, to Ranchi, back and forth. My beloved Madhulika, now worse, now better; I with a vague new life redolent of transitoriness; and Paro so bitter. From a courtroom to the office; from winding, wind-beaten roads to Panditji's House; from the typing class I had been forced to join to my aunt's yellow room; from the traffic infested lanes to the little shops I browsed in—I wandered back and forth wondering why I was so pleased to be dissatisfied with myself.

With myself as well as with everyone else around. Paro was relentless and importunate, making endless allusions to my disloyalty, to my lack of purpose in life, to my losing sight of my destination. Pratap was not behaving like himself; neither uncle, nor boss, nor friend, nor all three at once, as tightly knotted as his tie and as correct, bestowing the same smile on my aunt as on myself. The wick catching fire often trembles first in the flare of the match that is burning itself out. We begin before we begin to be finished and life goes on endlessly substituting for itself and who can tell where the break occurs? How can you foresee it? What can you remember that warrants confessions? Is our conduct explained as readily as we suppose by those tremendous scenes that memory has composed so dramatically for our private use, the snapshots that no one ever sees? But everyone makes his own outward landmarks, and I would like to point out a few of my own.

First of all the corridors of the high court. The clerks chew paan and leer at me: *"Kya maal hai!"* Then face to face with Thakur Sahib, the father, "You are working for Pratap, I am told. Good! You look lovely, my dear." And he actually pats my head while Pratap looks on, his face like a thundercloud. Thakur Sahib does not even ask after his daughter-in-law. Pratap says I need not go with him to the court again.

Then there is the yellow room. I have just come back from Ranchi, gone into the house ahead of Pratap, who has to put the car away. Paro scarcely notices I am home and goes on calculating her chances of getting out the queen of hearts in her patience spread out on Madhu's quilt. And Madhu, who is a little better today, puts down her novel to ask a thousand petty questions: What did we have for lunch? Did we have a client along? Is Pratap eating well? Did her friend from Brabourne College come to see Pratap about her land problem? Did I like my work? What is she afraid of? Every night she questions me like a fretful spy. Sometimes I blush for her when I think that we reserve for our intimates the same degree of confidence that we ourselves deserve; and sometimes, suddenly, noticing how she really looks, I decide that no husband in the world would be very much to blame if he were to deceive her now. And my sympathy balances between the two, cancelling itself out, so that I find neither my old long-cherished hope of watching their love die out nor even any regret at seeing it weakened, but instead a perverse kind of satisfaction in knowing them bound together so awkwardly, as well as an insurmountable repugnance at imagining my aunt replaced by another. But I need not trouble myself about that: I should know.

And on Madhu's birthday in January, out comes the large Dayarams box. Out tumble eleven gorgeous nightgowns, all in different shades of yellow, from the palest primrose to chrome and a yellow satin quilted robe embroidered with butterflies. "To match your setting, my dear," says Pratap.

Even Paro's eyes are wide and wet and I think, or rather catch myself short on the thought, How nice to have a husband like that. Madhu, smiling her vague, smile asks, "Do you think I'll never leave this room, then?"

A close if temporary harmony. All of us are too subjective for it to be anything else. Except Mala, and out of the blue she says as I am dressing for the office one morning, "You can't take what does not belong to you."

For a moment I think she is talking of things. "What do you mean?" I ask.

"Uncle Pratap," she says.

The sensitive husband is also subject to his moments of embarrassment. Mr. Prasad, one of his colleagues, walks into the office and, all smiles, says to me, "Mrs. Singh, I presume?"

"You do," say I. "Actually I am Mrs. Singh's niece. I work here."

So he shifts from *aap* to *tum*. "And what is your name?"
he asks.

"Friday," I answer, and flounce out of the office.

At Panditji's House, I would often find Pratap sitting at
Madhu's bedside while she slept under the heavy sedatives
we gave her to check the violent neuralgia that was almost
indistinguishable from the seizures of the original disease.
There sat Pratap, motionless, his elbows on his knees, his
face frozen in an expression of such anguish, such disgust,
such horrified expectancy, that I would throw myself
against my aunt's bed, shocked, furious, revolted at the
notion that I had actually wished them to break. But not
like this! All I had wanted was a decisive quarrel, a disillu-
sionment that would have sent Pratap away forever and put
us back to status quo. Was it only grief and fatigue I read
on his face? I sought in vain for traces of that old love of the
beautiful Madhu I had witnessed that first day as he handed
her on to the land from the boat. Sometimes I thought I
found it, but those times he was looking at me.

And Panditji's House seemed to resent me; every tree
twisted by the violent March winds protested at my treach-
ery. They would bend to the right, straighten up, then bend to
the left, saying, No . . . no . . . no . . . It was the voice of the
house itself I seemed to hear when Paro in one of her moods
shouted, "You're going bad! It's this town life. It gives you
hot blood!" Or when she tried to win me back murmuring,
"You used to be proud of this house once, Chchanda, you
used to love it; if you let it go, it is like cutting off a limb. . . ."

I still loved it. Sometimes at the office, I wondered what I was doing. Selling my soul for orange lipstick and handbags? I missed the air, the horizon, the movement of things around Panditji's House. I walked up and down the blue-grey carpet—no twigs to snap underfoot, no pebbles to kick, no mud to squish between my toes.

Once it got so bad, about the middle of March, I couldn't stand it anymore. Pratap was in court. I left a note on his pad and took a long and expensive ride in a taxi to Netarhat. Paro welcomed me with a great show of affection; told me how she had trimmed the roots of the bougainvillea bonsai just that morning. At eight-fifteen when Pratap came home, he found me swabbing my throat. I gallantly struck my colors: my tonsils, gums, and palate were so painted over with methylene that you couldn't see anything but blue. "Tonsillitis," said Paro.

Pratap believed us and gave me a week off. But by the fourth day, tired of wandering along the banks of the Koel or on the paths in the woods, unable to relive my old rustic joys, I returned to work. And the time went by. Went by. The Koel flowed tumultuously from the grove near Thakur Sahib's farm, ran fast with the short spring rains and dashed for the underground channel that led to the Suvarnarekha river. I felt underground too. Later I learned that the word for my feelings was "pathological," and something was bringing me very fast to a near and nasty revelation.

Chapter 13

It was the night between the twenty-fourth and twenty-fifth of March. About eleven-thirty. A grating sound, almost a groan, roused me from a nightmare in which I was Lord Dufferin who had once seen a ghost. But lords don't groan even in nightmares and the peculiar logic that lies in wait for even the most fantastic of our dreams, quiescent until some minor detail forces it to act upon us, forced me to wake from one terror only to be faced with another. Was my aunt worse? Was Paro snoring so loudly she could not hear the sound of the death-rattle? And not until I felt the rough carpet under my feet was I wide awake enough to recover my old ability to identify every noise in the house: that was it. The door to the woodshed had been left open and it was creaking on the rust of its own hinges, swinging back and forth in the draughts of a now tired wind.

I'd better get up and stop it from waking the rest of the house, I thought. The switch was under my fingers but I didn't turn it on. I've always loved prowling about this old house, stealthily groping my way along the walls. Once again my bare feet, as sensitive as my hands, recognized the places in the floor where the cement was scratchy, the worn spot on the landing. Down the stairs, skip the sixth one. With my big toe I found the row of tiles that three generations of passage have worn down between the furniture fixed in place by three generations of people's presence—a path leading from the front door to the kitchen. Out through the kitchen, almost into the backyard. But there I stopped short, so startled that I must have cried out aloud: facing me in the outer doorway trembled a disc of light and within it a hand held out towards the catch of the outer kitchen door.

"Chchanda, is that you? Did you come down because of the door too?" I recognized Pratap's voice, which went on, "Are you trying to play hide and seek? Why don't you turn on the light?"

"Why don't you, Pratap?"

The flashlight suddenly shone straight in my eyes and Pratap's voice was nearer, hoarser. "But you are wearing only a thin slip! No wonder you get tonsillitis. Go on, get upstairs to bed, I've closed the woodshed door tightly."

I stepped back, chilled and embarrassed, the light still in my eyes. I suddenly recalled the tales of Roman Catholic saints that Paro was so fond of telling us. I had the odd notion that, in my slip, with the light shining through my hair in a sort of aureole, I must look like a holy virgin about to be martyred for the faith.

"Go on now," said my executioner, seizing me by the arm. His fingers pressed tightly and the circle of light advanced before us, grazing the kitchen tiles, the legs of the table, the hooves of the range, the hinges of a crockery chest; the light landed here and there in utter confusion. At last it disappeared into Pratap's palm after snatching from our time-old things a bit or piece of their share of darkness and stripping them all of their genteel modesty. Now Pratap's fingers glowed red and translucent. He murmured as if to explain, "I remember when I was a child across the river," pointing in the direction of his father's house, "there were no lights, no electricity. I used to prowl around for hours, making things come out of the dark with my flashlight. I used to call it photography in reverse. But you must be freezing! Good night."

Good night, Pratap. Since the truce it is customary that you pat my cheek or shoulder and even though I am shivering, so thinly dressed, we might as well observe it now. But the flashlight misses its target and in the darkness, the fatherly pat aims haywire, landing on a breast, the place where I am just beginning to grow taut.

"Madhuchchanda!"

My name, but not my name alone. Whispered almost in my ear, so that I can feel the breath of it, and the smell of toothpaste and tobacco; a breath that burns my skin, suddenly harsh. Where is the torchlight? The hand that was holding it must have put it down somewhere, for the hand is now being used to hold my left arm down. Now, when

I should be struggling against him, bristling with outrage and screaming for Paro, I can manage only a barely audible "Let me go, Pratap, let me go!"

But the darkness takes me in his arms. His mouth is on mine, which already softens under the invading pressure and his knee moves between mine. "Madhuchchanda, Madhuchchanda!" and that is all he can say between the kisses that penetrate my lips like a hot seal into wax. All he can say and much too much!

Besieged from every side, and on every side surrendering, overwhelmed, aroused, knocked against the corner of the dresser, his victim too murmurs "Pratap!"

In my head, of course, runs the stupid thought, I should have put on my dressing gown. But would its old burgundy velvet have served so much better than thin cotton to defend what is barely able to resist, what must capitulate anyway in a sudden and sought-for defeat? Can this be me? Once so stiff with disapproval, now twisted, thrown down, riven by this astonishing pleasure, surprising Pratap even more than myself, so that now he falls upon me like a woodcutter, hurling his body against mine with the violence of an axe on the kitchen floor, subsiding at last on my shoulder, gasping, "Madhuchchanda, we must be mad! I didn't even take care of . . ."

You are right, Pratap, we must be mad. But what should you take care of? Of whom? The only chastity left to me now, from whom your pleasure so delicately detaches itself, will be the chastity that is willing to face the consequences.

It is the other Chchanda that you will have to take care of
now, the child you said "good night" to without making it
clear you meant "good-bye," the child you and I will never
see again. But I implore you, Pratap, stop saying "Madhuchchanda, Madhuchchanda!" The last part of it you used to
bray like a call to arms, now interwoven with a tender
stupidity. If you only knew how much I would give at this
moment to be called just "Gita" or "Rita" or "Bina" or
"Mina"! For the first part of my name is one you have
panted a hundred times into another ear. "Madhu" is also
a woman lying upstairs whose transgressions have more
claim upon you than mine.

"Let me go, no, let me go!"

"My love, don't go."

I stagger upstairs, one strap of my slip torn. I stumble
twice in the darkness; step on the sixth stair. This is a house
where I once knew my way by instinct: a house that
doesn't know me anymore.

Chapter 14

I woke very early the next morning, angry for having been able to sleep, incredulous that I had slept at all. Was it true then, was it even possible? The broken strap of my slip exposing one breast and the two drawn bolts on the door left me no excuse to doubt last night's reality. Breathless and afraid of being pursued to our room itself, I had locked the door and stood over Mala, making sure that she was sleeping soundly and uninterruptedly, lighting furtive matches over her face and dropping them, half-burnt, by the side of the bed. Finally, rolling myself into a ball, cupping all my limbs around the central wound that suddenly had become so light and yet so deep as to leave me forever indefensible, I lay on my bed like a wild animal—teeth, fists, and eyelids clenched, incapable of moving, or thinking, or understanding, pulling my head farther down between my shoulders each time the chowkidar in the square rang his time-gong. I must have dozed off, nevertheless. A rooster clearing his throat on one of the river farms wakened me.

A dingy light filled the open window, diluted the faded pink of the carpet between Mala's bed and mine. Mala was sleeping as she had slept all night, as she would always sleep, fallen under her own feather-weight, which was still only hers, still intact, reproaching me for not being able to keep to myself even this little piece of concealed and central flesh.

And suddenly my body slackened. I smacked one hand against the other to catch a mosquito where I thought I heard its faint humming. I missed it and it disappeared towards the ceiling. Mala opened both eyes and closed them again. Trampling on last night's slip I rushed to get dressed with a passion to cover my whole body that made me put on layer upon layer of clothes, not satisfied until I had on thick jeans, a thick sweater, and a long muffler wound round and round my neck in the comfortable warmth of March. Thus armored, I risked creeping down the stairs and then throwing myself out-of-doors.

The sharpness of the air that matched the shrewish temper of the little birds fluttering in the grass seemed to do me good. A bluish mist composed of moisture and woodsmoke covered the slope to the river, stuffing the clearings with cotton, filling them as high as the surrounding branches of the peepul trees. Though the sun was not yet in sight, the East quickly dominated the colorless sky, the light ricocheting from cloud to cloud and at last getting entrapped by the black-branched, leafless palas, the tree we called the flame of the forest in our parts. I walked woodenly, bruising the simul flowers underfoot, those blameless, tiny blossoms of white with orange stalks. One day, I thought, I would have a pair of earrings like the simul flower in coral and pearl; one day, some day, if I ever was a whole person again. Now I walked, a leaden statue. Unhesitatingly, I continued towards the river. My only feeling was a sense of astonishment that the landscape, the air, and the light should all be just as they usually were, as faithful as ever to themselves. Ignoring the path, I walked purposely through the clumps of weeds where the dew ran down my ankles and began to soak into my sandals. By the time I reached the Guatemala grass on the river's edge, I was running hard. The muddy line that the river had etched with the March floods covered an old nick on a teak tree from which Paro hoped to make money. I couldn't see clearly today but the bark had a commemorating date that I knew by heart: Madhulika, 1938.

Madhuchchanda, 1952, ran down the bank and came to the water's edge near the landing bend, that detestable place where Pratap and Madhu had landed a lifetime ago, a place still covered with a dull slime that the height of summer would dry. There was the upthrust of a great army of reeds but there was no choice and no hesitation. My muffler unrolled itself, the sweater fell inside out, the sleeves spread absurdly empty and all the rest flung anywhere and anyhow. I plunged into the water, at last recovering something of what I had lost, surfacing, beating my arms against the foam, against the current, against myself while the cold greedily gnawed my skin.

At the end of my strength and out of breath, I climbed out of the water just as the sun appeared, a spreading long streak of red against the grey horizon. Naked, but without much consideration for my charms, I rubbed myself with my vest until the skin burnt, regretting that I had not the courage to do it with nettles, and by the time I had put on my outfit again, I was almost stifled by its weight. The river fog had thinned and disappeared in sinuous gutters and winding paths, reminding me of my own complex thoughts. But it was no easier for me to gossip with myself than with anyone else. I had to bait myself to wheedle explanations: You have a lover. You have slept with your uncle. And that was all I could get, all I could use to threaten that affected girl inside me who, though she recoiled at my uncompromising words, refused, nevertheless, to perish with her own virtue.

Leaving the riverbank, I walked straight on, and at last, after three or four complete circuits of Panditji property, I allowed myself to collapse on the old stump that had been my throne since I was small. If Pratap was not exactly my uncle, having come on the scene too late for real acceptance or relationship, I was nevertheless his mistress. I didn't love him of course and he certainly didn't love me. He had simply given in to a meaningless temptation, taken advantage of one of those stupid moments of weakness that several novels assured me overcame a woman's resistance as they overcame (hadn't I, a country-bred girl, seen it many times?) goats and cats and cows. It was regrettable, deplorable: but there it was. I had lost my virginity in the way you lose an arm or an eye: by accident.

The image brought me up short. In my rage of self-humiliation, I had gone too far. I jumped up, suddenly tired of punishing myself, disguisted by my own insults. An exact recollection of the night before flamed in my cheeks and for about five burning moments, the "accident" seemed quite a different matter. Blind, yes, we had been blind and we had agreed to look away from the truth—our eyelids had fallen with a single accord. But far back, for days, weeks now, a fire had been smouldering under the wicked ashes. Pratap's sudden greedy glances, those hesitant light touches of his hand, stumbling over words when we were alone in the office, the very pressure and patience with which he had laid siege—were not all these indications as exact as my own ill-natured coquetry: an eagerness to wage the fragile wars in which my own aggression had doubtless never been anything but a mask of jealousy?

If we had been restrained, inhibited, something in us both had broken free at last, and we had yielded, mutually surprised, mutually shaken to our passions.

To passions! The word was soothing, it excused everything, charged as it was with the unexplored mysteries, unknown, nocturnal fatalities, less flowery perhaps, but more violent than love. I repeated it five or six times without even noticing that I had passed from anger to effusion. From one sentimentality to another. My furies counterattacked: "A passion"—don't flatter yourself. What are you going to do with all your fine feelings, your determination to keep Panditji's property to yourself, your aunt, your sister, and your Paro. After all, Pratap is a married man. Of course, that sort of question would worry only an inexperienced girl and you could hardly claim that status anymore—you lost it without much fuss and no concern for the civil status of your accomplice. So why are you twisting yourself around your little sin but all the same being very careful not to uncover what is really important? He is not only married, he's married to your aunt, that invalid upstairs who loves you and also loves this gentleman. Of course, to be seduced in thirty seconds, when you have the reputation of being such a shrew, is rather a nasty blow, but to be seduced by the only man you haven't the right to touch, that is the real black, the little incest, that even a cold bath in the Koel will not wash out of your system, and your conscience.

"Chchanda, where are you?" shouted someone from the house. I ran off in the opposite direction. The grounds were too small. I jumped over an embankment and ran off along Satpals's Plain—a big pasture owned by one of my grandfather's friends, a Sikh now settled in Ranchi. It was rented out in acre lots and dotted with clots of old cowdung as hard as biscuits. The voice followed, "Chchanda. Where are you? . . . It's time for . . ."

Another voice that had no need of passing through my ears followed me too. "Run, run," it said, "get hold of yourself a little. We've plenty of things to talk over still. Have you thought that you would never have scored such a victory over your aunt, if she had not been disfigured? You're young enough all right, and something new. After all your knees are well oiled and your breasts hard. But you can't offer much besides freshness, really, certainly not your aunt's beauty or charisma—and to tempt the devil with what little you have, he has to have gone without it for a while. You're in a fair way to lose it when Madhulika gets well."

And just at that moment, my sweater caught. I turned around with a muffled scream, but it was only a briar. I looked at my water-soaked wristwatch, which was the only item I had forgotten to remove during my plunge into the Koel: a bubble wagged back and forth between the frozen hands as if it were a level, the little hand at four, the minute hand, ten minutes before. It must be after seven by now. The shouts began again and there at the other end of the field was Pratap, his briefcase under his left arm, shouting and waving, right arm over his head.

My legs turned to stone as I watched him come towards me. I noticed with irritation how he stretched his all too regular stride to avoid the patches of cowdung—they were hardly the steps of a man who was overwhelmed by what he had done the night before, he was not fooling himself that it was rape. Since waking I had been dreading this moment—divided between the desire to meet him with all my claws out and the impulse to dissolve into tears on his shirtfront. When he was still several yards off and I saw him glance at the bushes on the edge of the field that might have concealed God-knows-what spies, my distress and my hostility managed to combine a still third attitude: Be natural and nothing more; then the ball will be in his court.

But Pratap, doubtless to avoid both claws and sentimentality, cried out a command, "It's only seven-fifteen but hurry up! I think this morning it would be best to start early. So change and say good-bye to Madhulika, and fast!" All this loudly, and softly, "I won't kiss you now. Paro is watching."

Not one question; not one remark. His methods were certainly consistent in every situation: circumspection, discretion, and a little salve on secret wounds. His face showed nothing at all—not desire, not triumph, not uneasiness. It was an everyday face. But he whispered, "Get yourself in hand, Chchanda, I beg of you. Your face will give everything away—we'll have to be very careful from now on!"

Chchanda. So what happened to Madhuchchanda? The complicity of the bushes we were walking through didn't seem to give him much confidence, not even a notion that he might put his arm around me. Was he afraid of startling me, or had he decided that such things would be all too easy in the darkness of the kitchen or at the office-apartment? Had he already organized our madness, assigned it to its place in his schedule and his peace of mind? I knew that he was one of those people who have a real confectioner's genius for wrapping up the nastiest facts in the sweetest appearances. But I was impressed by his calm and confidence too, and I let myself follow him with a certain amount of relief. Reaching the house, I changed quickly. Pratap had the car ready. "Did you see Madhulika?" he asked.

"No."

"I think you are right. Let's just get away. You probably aren't feeling up to breakfast: anyway, that's what I told Paro. As a matter of fact I was very hungry." With that piece of euphemism Pratap turned the car on to the road for Ranchi driving at about seventy miles an hour. The speed indicated the limits of his assurance: In the Ambassador, at least, we had nothing to fear; he could, he should, have found the sort of phrases that would have comforted me, calmed my fears. But he said nothing at all, this Pratap, hunched over the wheel as if he were driving over precipices. From time to time came out a small snort, too consciously stripped of any meaning or intention. It was ridden with a false embarrassment that hoped to set me off the scent and gain a little time for himself.

We were passing the beautiful grounds of Our Lady of Fatima convent just outside Ranchi when Pratap said, "That's where Mala is going to lodge."

"To lodge?"

"Yes, you know Rev. Mother Gertrude?"

I did. She was at the Ursuline Convent at Netarhat for a

while and had taken keenly to Mala. Furthermore, Thakur Sahib had donated a large piece of land without buildings to the nuns.

"She has agreed," continued Pratap, "that Mala can live here and attend Loreto School. She will travel the short four miles to Ranchi with Rev. Mother Xavier, who—apart from being the departmental head of English at St. Xavier's College—also takes the advanced students for two hours of English. She is the only American nun in this zone and her forefathers founded Fordham University. I took some of Mala's essays to her. Has Mala ever shown you them?"

"No. Has my aunt agreed?"

"Of course."

All this I heard through a haze, my main concern being my own destiny.

Once in his office everything changed. I already suspected what he had in mind. No matter how great a sin may be, it loses most of its heinousness if you repeat it often enough; it wears out whatever remorse you have started out with feeling. A girl taken twice is hardly a girl taken by surprise, and seduction is a poor argument when continuous. After all, what better comment on love than love; especially when it is forbidden and its only hope is to invade the blood itself? The office door barely shut behind us before Pratap took me into his arms and gave me a long, suffocating kiss. He had to break off, of course, to cancel all his appointments, but that was over in three minutes. I was crouched in the chair-for-important-clients, waiting to tell him how disgusting we had been, that I didn't want this job anymore, and where would it all end? What were we going to do . . . "Make love," said Pratap.

Already my struggling hands were overcome by a detestable joy that began to act like opium, against all resistance. What can a lamb, suddenly hemmed in by a panther, do against its foe? And why lie to oneself?

Pratap was not the only panther in that tiny office. At the supreme moment when any argument was good enough, he used the truest: "Never mind, Madhuchchanda, the worst is over. Why spoil the rest?"

Chapter 15

It was time to go home and Pratap drove us back over the same road with the same serious intensity. Yet in his every gesture was a new reassurance, a kind of confident repose. For the time being he had conquered: I asked for nothing more than silence. Doubtless we were still far from the warm complicity, the arrogant indifference towards the rest of the universe that shields the famous lovers of history, whether their passion's right to exist has been challenged or not. Our particular business had scarcely ceased being a matter of bodies, interrupted by one uncertain truce after another, during which Pratap seemed to lose his advantage, not knowing how to defend himself against my remorse except by drowning it, over and over again, in a sea of pleasure. But he had also succeeded in silencing what remained in me of yesterday's virgin, stifled now in her ecstatic shame, stupefied at recovering her former modesty together with the bitter recognition, the tenderness of her whole flesh, the very joy of drawing breath with another

body that has just revealed to you the insistence of your
own. I had become his mistress. I could no longer be igno-
rant of all that had pushed me into his arms, and now
confronted by the magnitude of the disaster—which,
miraculously as it seemed at times, remained no less a
disaster—I had only one desire: to shut out all afterthoughts,
all knowledge, all awareness of what was to come, by
closing my eyes and clasping my arms tightly around me.

Like Pratap after all. I was no longer deceived by his
seriousness or his calm: we all have our masks. Abandoning
to others the kind that grimaces, he had chosen for his own
one of the most serene; he tied on an ease of manner that
had become quite habitual, and you had to know him very
well, had to look very closely to discover, in moments of
strain, the effort he was making to keep it on straight,
betrayed only by light parallel wrinkles that showed like
guitar strings on his forehead.

By the last turn of the road those little wrinkles had run
down to the corners of his eyes and then we had reached
Panditji's House. He turned badly, and had to back up twice
before we got into the garage—our old onions and potato
shed, where he stood for a while, his head under the hood,
supposedly checking the oil gauge and the brake fluid.
Maybe he thought I would run in without him, now that
he had taught me something about being bold; that I would
repay his pains by sparing him the ticklish drudgery of
restoring the strayed lamb to her aunt. But I didn't budge
from his elbow, of course, partly due to cowardice, partly

from resentment, leaving it up to him to suggest that we run away, or make a scene so that the choice of refusal would be mine. Finally, he straightened up, gallant as ever. "In we go," he announced.

Indoors I could hear Paro slamming her cupboards and screaming at Mala, "You! You've brought out all those moth-eaten books, for what? And who is going to dust . . ."

At least I knew where she was. I tiptoed past the kitchen, stepping over heaps of books in the hallway; deciding it would be better, since I had left without saying good-bye, to come in without any greeting either. No opportunity for reproaches or scrutiny. Expressionless, the little lady comes and goes, and if she neglects her dear family a bit, surely her dear family will forgive her—after all she works so hard, she commutes to Ranchi, and both ways it is over eighty miles. And she works not only for money but is with her uncle at one of the toughest times a man can know. Poor girl, she needs her rest.

I began to climb the stairs, Pratap shadowing me. Once we were at the landing, he grasped my arm, "Don't you think it would be better if we went in to see your aunt one by one? I don't want to give her the feeling that we are in league."

And you don't want to lie too much in front of me, I added mentally, or to let me watch you bestowing your customary gallantries. There was something satisfying in outguessing Pratap and in surprising him.

His eyes met mine and for a moment the old hostile look

was in them, whatever yielding the rest of my body may have done. He straightened his shoulders, "Come on, you little fool!"

But his shoulders fell again as soon as he heard Madhulika protesting: "There you are, you two. I thought I had been completely abandoned!"

I rushed towards her, suddenly freed of all my fear—this was not a feeling I need be afraid of in front of anyone. I didn't have to pretend to be feeling it or worry if the feeling was offending anyone. I could kiss this woman who had been father and mother, guide and confessor to me, but now I was kissing her with lips still warm from another kind of kiss.

Pratap blurted out his customary "How are you now"—itself an equivocation. He watched us stiffly, as Madhu and I exchanged our caresses, trying out a painful smile that betrayed his every apprehension. How could he behave decently towards one of us without feeling he was behaving improperly towards the other? One corner of my mind was a little sorry for him. But I had noticed how troubled Madhu's breathing had become, her color purplish, and there was a loud wheezing in her lungs. As I curled almost around Madhu, trying to give her my own robust strength, Pratap must have stood there and wondered what to make of this niece who had gloried in her scrupulousness all morning, only to return and curl catlike on the breast of her beloved rival.

"I am sorry about this morning, Madhu. We had to leave

early, we had an appointment; you were still asleep."

"You never said anything about an appointment," said Madhu, whose eyes wandered towards my own, seeking confirmation.

But the word "appointment" and what it concealed brought the blood to my face. The sudden notion that my aunt might interpret my embarrassment scarcely served to diminish it, and Pratap crowned everything in his efforts to disentangle us, "It's something to do with a tribal having sold land to a domiciled Bengali," he said, making everything very clear. "I am going downstairs for a while to work on it." And the traitor slipped out.

Who could understand better than I how untenable the situation was for him, what reactions he was trying to control, to provoke. Ungratefully enough, I reproached him as much for the very consideration he exercised on my behalf at Madhu's expense, as if he had sacrificed my feelings for her sake, thereby refusing to show his preference for a girl all too sure of herself to need such a display, and, in fact, not at all sure she wasn't deriving a dreadful little joy in the very worst corner of her black heart from the whole exhibition.

Confusion is a bad inspiration and I put my arm lightly around my aunt as she sighed, "Poor Pratap, it's not very easy for him. He tries so hard, but I think he's getting tired of the whole thing. I'm glad you are with him so much. The very drive from here to Ranchi . . ." Her very confidence struck at my throat and I realized that from now on, the least phrase, the merest word, would reach its target, would wound someone, bear a dubious, inevitably offensive interpretation. My nails dug into the yellow quilt. Even when there was darkness out, this room looked full of sunshine. That was Madhu for you. Beautiful of face, beautiful of mind, beautiful of taste. Then pity, pity for all of us, ran through me like knives and I wept as that voice continued to pour out its intolerable sweetness, "The way I look now, you know, I am not under any illusions. And Pratap wouldn't be much to blame. . . ."

Not much to blame; I had thought so once. But I couldn't let myself admit it anymore without degrading myself to the level of the occasion—the easiest expedience of all. My spite turned me inside out, like a sock; how a woman betrays herself by such a weak and yet such a tolerant view of men! Even though I told myself that such apparent indulgence, put to the test, would burst out in accusations like the merest jealousy, I couldn't bear the thought. But why should she say such things, and at this moment of all? What lay under these gentle sentences? Some terrifying divination, or just the simple-minded cunning of an invalid whose imagination is overactive? I must put an end to it right away; no tears, no scene, no tirade.

"Look Aunt Madhu, we have enough troubles already to need to invent new ones. Don't make up such ridiculous ideas."

"Ridiculous? Do you think so, Chchanda?"

I decided to be brutal: "Are you trying to say that, while

I am in the office, Pratap is sleeping around someplace in town, or when I am out on errands, he is bringing someone to sleep there?"

No reaction. Her hand dropped slowly from my hair to my chin: a caress for the innocent child. She scarcely needed to tell me what she was thinking. That good little girl, that Chchanda, was still too young to see farther than her stubby eyelashes, too nice to upset her aunt even if she noticed something, but too clumsy as well, too easily disturbed by the slightest secret to hold it back by blustering. As long as she protested so loudly, so baldly, there was probably nothing to worry about.

"Pour me some tea, Chchanda, will you? I have some things to say to you."

I poured the tea, now cold and bitterly infused; my heart thudded so loudly, I was sure Madhu could hear it. She drank the tea in two gulps, so thirsty. That meant fever and another crisis. And this was the moment she had chosen.

Contrite, woebegone, an executioner dancing attendance upon his victim.

"About Paro," continued my aunt, "she must always have a home here. That goes without saying. My father's— your grandfather's—friend, Jaipal Singh, brought her here. Not a servant; a member of the family."

"She is that, isn't she?"

"Yes. But smooth the path between her and Pratap always. Actually, Thakur Sahib understands her status better than Pratap does. Look after Paro. I can't just now."

"Yes," I replied, tears again in my voice.

"Mala will get a good education. My God! How little you both have had from me." A longish silence.

"By the way, what was Pratap saying about tribal property and its sale?"

This was safer and I could reply: "A man called Deven Sunrao, of the Oaroan tribe, sold a piece of land to a Bengali. As you know, tribals are not allowed to sell land to non-tribals without the sanction of the state government. So now the Bengali has neither his land nor his money, and Sunrao has both."

I had made up the details on the spur of the moment (such cases were a way of life anyway). Now all I had to do was to warn Pratap. Then I began to wonder. Madhu's insistence exasperated me. It seemed scarcely appropriate to question me about these things. My role was certainly not that of a spy on my uncle's transgressions. And this little resentment, silly as it was, helped me out of all proportion to its significance, in the way that any pretext we can find helps us against those who have more than a pretext to hold against us. (At the bottom of the heap, barely recognized or formulated, lay the blackest excuse of all: What Madhu had done to us by marrying Pratap, I had repaid by taking him as a lover.)

And finally, I yielded to my despondency. From now on I wouldn't have to be on my guard night and day, taking incessant precautions in a forest of hints, implications, and double meanings. I decided I had put myself to the test sufficiently for the first time, and with the excuse that I hadn't seen Paro or Mala since I had come in, I ran out of Madhu's room.

My uncle-in-law was not in his room downstairs. I found him in the living room where, determined to halve the work of good relationships all round, he was gravely unwrapping a Cadbury bar for Mala and no less seriously consulting Paro about our fruit and rose grafting. Wasn't this the right time for grafting the guavas? Our own trees yielded so little and he had noticed some fine stocks growing wild in the woods, the pink-fleshed kind.

Shaking her head and not pausing a moment in setting out wiped *thalis* and *katoras* on the table, Paro protested in the name of all the ancient customs, which she had worked up into an exact science, "No, impossible, scions won't 'take' in a leap year."

Well, what about the mulberry bushes? Same thing. Can't do anything before the Feast of St. Ignatius of Loyola, the thirty-first of July.

What about the papaya trees! Have to plant one female next to one male and can't tell these things beforehand.

A harmless conversation, like the ones my grandmother and Paro used to have: "Don't tie a *rakhi* when there is a *grahan.*" Paro, a sniff: "These Brahmins!"

Paro: "You don't chew the wafer of the Holy Communion. It is Christ's flesh and blood."

Nani: "Bloody unlikely" (but very softly).

Don't sow under a crescent moon; it will be ready to reap

before you are. When the cuckoos sing, the maize is ripe and so on. Unfortunately, I was reminded of still another of these sayings of my grandmother and Paro: "If he doesn't drink and he doesn't limp and he falls down anyway, there's something wrong with his heart."

Paro pretended not to see me, she was hard to make out, harder to provoke, distant, or perhaps just being careful, I couldn't tell. I tried to make it easier for them to make their conversation go smoothly, only unfortunately, I had been thinking of the last proverb, "If Pratap doesn't drink and he doesn't limp and he falls down anyway, ha . . . ha . . . ha . . . if he doesn't drink . . . ha . . . ha . . . ha . . ." I went on and on laughing with tears streaming down my face. The three looked at me in stunned silence.

Mala edged closer, "Chchanda, you are not feeling well, too tired. Come upstairs to bed. I'll bring you some milk."

"My baby, my baby!" and I was engulfed in Paro's arms.

Pratap stared after us, as I was borne upstairs. I am sure his greatest fear was that I would confess everything hysterically on Paro's flat chest.

Chapter 16

If the hybrid-rose called the "blue moon" is what you need and you can't find it, the common chira-basant (spring-forever) of the same color will do as well, and provide the very same excuses for sentimentality: You have your magnificent miseries; you add your name to the list of doomed passions—so brief but so intense; you take your place among the privileged lovers who have tried to make a heaven out of hell.

Yet Pratap was the kind of man who found it difficult to think of himself as a star-crossed lover, the hero of a dark romance, and you would have surprised him a good deal if you told him that he had just accomplished with his niece what Phaedra had so utterly botched with her stepson or Oedipus achieved so successfully with his mother. Paro used always to say that Thakur Sahib had nothing in his house but law books and what can you learn out of them? Certainly not about incest. Even I had to admit that my brief happiness, my six-days' rapture, had so far affected me more like a seesaw than anything else, sometimes mounting to the skies, sometimes sinking to Hades, so that I wavered forever between indescribable sensations of dizziness and nausea.

Six days and a few hours to be exact. It ended in a grey smudge. Pratap came down to dinner with the announcement that my aunt's temperature had risen to 104: we were beginning to accustom ourselves to these sudden rises that discouraged Dr. Bose so much, and the news was rather a help. Our guilt and embarrassment during dinner could pass for worry.

But Paro's attitude worried me more than ever now. I never liked to see her lower those uncompromising jaws, screwing her neck into her shoulders—she was usually active, so generous in her movements. But she would speak only to Mala, look only at Mala, whom she criticized all the time: a spot of gravy on her sleeve, opened books everywhere, oh just anything. A high wind was blowing this witch-ridden night, revealing the dark sky with splashes of violet lightning. I got up to stare out of the window. It was only March going out like the proverbial lion but it does so, so seldom in India; the vociferous heat engulfs all lions.

Paro suddenly roused herself from her sullen silence, "You like that, don't you? Damaged goods always love wrecks."

I decided not to help her in the kitchen. I went up to bed in a clean, darned, and ironed slip. None of it my work. Paro. It had been no ordinary tear.

That morning—it was Wednesday—Mala had to shake me awake: nature occasionally does us a favor. And this time it was Pratap who was in a bad way. It must have been his turn to spend the night thinking, trying to answer the questions that came instead of sleep. After hesitating to leave the house ("Your aunt is really worse today, I'd like to know what Dr. Bose thinks, but we are so behind with our work"), we finally left for the office and called at Dr. Bose's on the way out of Netarhat, asking him to go by Panditji's House. For the rest of the morning Pratap presented me with an interesting picture of a man cut in two. For Mr. Singh, the lawyer, there was the usual program—the serious approach, the almost-reasonable look that things assume if you only look at them reasonably enough, if you revive your courage by confining your attention to the routine. But at the same time, this son of Wagner scraped away at his soul and evidently regretted not being able to salve his wounds with self-justification.

As we walked in, after several little formalities at the tip of his tongue, he said, "Now, Girl Friday, let's get down to work!" But once two of his clients had been taken care of, Girl Friday suddenly found herself on his knees, while that gentleman stammered, "Come now, let's be serious, come on!" Almost immediately these twinges of conscience subsided to be replaced by the dovelike accents of flirtation, the interesting explorations of sexual busybodies. We tried everything—irony towards the gentleman: If this continues, this office will never recover. And you are responsible to

Thakur Sahib to an extent, crown prince. And irony towards the lady, who was scarcely pleased and yet scarcely
sorry to learn that the prisoner in the tower, quite alive
after all, was humming away beneath her with a certain
gleam in his eye, "If my father knew about this, Madhuchchanda . . ." And finally, in spite of irony, in spite of
seriousness, came the surrender, "My work can wait a little
longer."

Work had already waited and waited. Pratap would go
out to attend to it, his head high with righteousness, come
back a little later, his head down. I could see how undecided
he was, how anxious to sweep away his scruples, to assert
his right to pleasure. And although I was a little humiliated
by so many requirements, I was woman enough already to
discern the trap in which the lover who believes he pos-
sesses is himself possessed, and to let Pratap take his pleasure with me—in a brief but so sensual accord that I almost
had the feeling, I was taking advantage of him. Less docile
in between these spasms, I lay in wait like a cat before a
mouse-hole, watching closely for the moment when he
would let himself go, when his real feelings would force his
hand.

Finally, around twelve, he said, while tying his necktie
again, "Dear God, Madhuchchanda, what's happening to
us? We are a scandal, you and I!" And his voice became
magnificently hoarse as he added, "But I couldn't care less.
I give a damn. I can't do without you."

For a moment—the best yet—it all seemed so clear, simple, luminous even. I knew it all now and there was nothing to be said. I was willing to take the rest for granted. He loved me, I loved him as much as it was possible for me to love, and before any judge in the world we could plead the legality of our love, which preceded all others. That Pratap was practically my guardian, or that I was practically his ward, was only a detail and though a village jury might choose to emphasize this detail, it was still just an accident that he saw Madhulika across the river first while I was still growing up. First of all he was Pratap, just as first of all I was Madhuchchanda. We were before everything else, Madhuchchanda and Pratap. Full stop. The universe would have to get used to it.

"I should have married you," said Pratap regretfully.

And spoiled it all. The kill-joy angel that watched over me extended the shadow of his wings, darkening my exultation and crying: Hear that? So you believe in miracles, do you? The advantage of the kind of lie you are telling yourself is that you try and prove it isn't a lie at all by toppling over all your meager principles and vast prejudices and suddenly pouring yourself a new glass of philosophy. You condemn your aunt's marriage because it upsets your equanimity of life, you resent this man as an interloper; your aunt is sick and, somewhere at the back of your addled brain, you feel he is to blame. Yet you separate your village life from your office life and feel this Pratap is yours, whereas the other is your aunt's and owes her everything he is giving you. You resent him for her sake and gather into your own greedy arms what belongs to her. Remember how you felt about those yellow clouds of nightdresses? How would you have behaved if his mistress were anyone but you?

Pratap sighed suddenly, and at that moment, I hated him so much for that sigh that I couldn't stop myself from asking a question I had always longed to ask: "Why did you marry my aunt?"

He blinked several times in succession, avoiding my eyes, which grew miserable as his own embarrassment increased. "I want you to understand why," he said, half whispering, "but it will be hard for you, if not impossible. You would have to know what happened for a long time past—my childhood—and these two ethereal girls across the river, your mother and Madhulika. Your mother so haughty even at ten, Madhulika so *simpatico* to the little boy across the river. And you know, they both wore skirts with large Scottish checks, a large pin in the front. I used to think their mother must be very lazy not to stitch their clothes when torn. 'Panditji is letting things go slack. This is no life for him, he should go back to the city, he lacks stimuli here. He knows nothing about farming. They are getting dirt poor.' Poor? The fairy princesses poor? What did it matter? I can't think things clearly out. I was fascinated by those girls, nothing clearly and neatly defined. They were like a secret grotto in my mind, running water and flowers.

"You know where the water is narrowest and shallow-est, down by Dr. Markham's house? Your mother and Madhulika would jump from stone to stone there while I walked on the other side, pretending nonchalance, every nerve in my body aware of them. One day, Miss Elke said, 'Talk to them, Pratap, play with them. They are only a little older than you.' I ran from there. I was consumed with curiosity about how they lived, what they did. Then away at college, I met Kiron Mukherjee, or rather he deigned to talk to me. He was a graduate student then, worshipped for his charm and brilliance by students and professors alike. He had a place near here and was on the brink of a nervous breakdown. I suggested Netarhat as a place for rest. He married your mother here. Invaded part of the secret grotto. Above all, managed to marry your mother, the most unap-proachable of girls, whereas I dared not even speak to them. The marriage didn't work, as you know. Your mother wanted to get away with someone she could lean on; at the same time she was hard enough to push off anyone wanting to lean on her. I don't know how far you can remember, but Aparajita was even more beautiful than Madhulika."

"I've heard people say that, but go on."

"Many years after Aparajita's death, Madhu came to me for advice regarding many things—finances, guardianship, etc. When she walked into my office, I felt I was peeking at my grotto again. I could not do enough. Things bunch together, whether you want them to happen, or they hap-pen by themselves. This princess from my village, in my office—she must not go alone in a taxi, she must have a sunshade even if no other woman used one. Things slid, they happened, and I learned to accept that the fantasy of

Jita-Madhu across the river was gone forever—for here was
Madhu in the flesh. I can tell you now that I didn't want
to get married and Madhu pretended not to, either—because
of you girls or because of what people would say or because
she was just a little older than I. But she was desperately in
need of money and security. She changed her mind, almost
unnoticeably at first, mentioning it now and then, and then
again, a little more often. Then she thought she was pregnant, probably the first queasy symptoms of the lupus, and
neither of us had any other reason to consider."

"Shut up, Pratap," I cried, "don't say anymore."

And he stopped, knowing how little his sleepy voice
could account for my aunt's power over him, could con-
vince me that he was altogether mine now. I moved away
from him, suddenly alienated, sulky. Aparajita and Madhulika had so little to do with me. Pratap decided to make
an issue of it. "How quickly you change your feelings,
Chchanda."

"Not as fast as you change your women, Pratap," I
shouted, poisoning the rest of the day, which he preferred
to spend in court, draped in his black robes, the same way
as I wore my mood, relying, no doubt, on the virtues of a
first separation that isolates a bride so terribly, finally giving
her time for her lips to go quite dry.

As he left, he sped one last parting shot, "You are much
more like Aparajita than Madhu."

"Good," I shot back, "at least you were in awe of her."

On Thursday I was able to repay him. Dr. Bose had been

at Panditji's House the afternoon before and had left us a note in which he asked us to nurse the patient carefully. "Her heart is very troublesome," he had added. I made it a pretext to stay home for the day, and Pratap agreed to my proposal with disconcerting readiness, saying only, "It's a good idea, Chchanda, no one will suspect anything now." I found myself baffled by an opposition that I hoped would indicate how baffled Pratap was by mine. I also thought of him as shoddy; the affair cheap and underhand, all of which it was anyway. And he left for Ranchi alone. Paro couldn't believe her eyes. "Have you been quarrelling with that one?" she asked, half pleased, half annoyed—there has to be a certain amount of intimacy first, to quarrel with anyone. But she quickly recovered her sulks when I walked away without answering her. I hadn't told her I was planning to stay at home; torn between my affection and the fear her intransigence and loyalty inspired in me, I avoided all discussion with so dangerously far-sighted an opponent. Heartbroken by my own behavior, offending Paro more and more, I scarcely said anything to her these days, except a few formalities; I hardly knew how to behave with her anymore.

And my sister didn't make matters any better with her astute questions and remarks. "You get along remarkably well with Pratap these days, Chchanda."

"Isn't that what you wanted?"

"Oh yes! We eat better, wear better clothes, and look at what he is doing towards my education! And one has to pay

for what one gets out of life. Our aunt certainly isn't paying," said my angel-faced sister. She had outgrown me by
several inches and was statuesque to my skinniness. Now
she combined the wisdom of a Mother Superior and the
madame of a whorehouse in her expressive eyes.

"Mala," I asked, my heart in my mouth, "what do you
mean?"

She changed the subject. "I met Thakur Sahib last week-
end, walking in the woods. He asked how our aunt was."

"But I met him in town and he didn't ask me. Why?"

"The next time you meet him say, 'Wagner, you asked
my sister about our aunt, your daughter-in-law, but you
didn't ask me. Why?'" She was busy with a dress. "This
frock is for Mrs. Prabhakar's daughter, how do you like it?"

I fled from Mala. I fled from Paro. To Madhulika's room.

She was feeling weak but was quite conscious and immediately comforted by the treat. "You're going to stay with
me all day?"

"I'll stay on one condition . . . no talking."

I was afraid she would be insistent and worried and I
knew I could never face that. I resolved not to let myself be
moved or involved in her confidences, to confine myself,
instead, to the role of painstaking nurse, who firmly im-
poses her instructions: rest, silence.

It was more than I could manage. I was scarcely settled,
facing the bed, a book in my hand like a shield, when Paro
pounded into the yellow room and began fussing with the
medicine bottles that had replaced the perfumes and night

creams and moisturizers on Madhu's dressing-table. "Go on, read your love yarns," she hissed at me, "that's all you're good for!"

Feeling worthless, useless, and clumsy, I stuck to my guns and my chair. She bathed Madhu tenderly like a Magdalen, the fervor better than even that one's asking no help from me at all. Madhu didn't miss the trick, and her eyes looked startled in the middle of a face too scabbed over to express anything at all. She didn't say anything, but Paro somehow noticed all the same and became immediately ashamed. Her old tenderness surfaced. "I'll leave Chchanda with you," she crooned to Madhu in a good-natured tone quite belied by the violence with which she turned her back on me.

As soon as Paro had left, Madhulika murmured with a smile in her voice, like an accomplice, "Dear good Parvati! She can't forgive you for being nice to Pratap." And the inevitable happened. I closed the book. I brought my chair nearer the bed, a little nearer, nearer still, right up next to it. "But she ought to see by now," continued Madhu, "she ought to know him better—he's such a nice person. . . ." and the eulogies of Pratap began, a kind of singsong chant, broken by sudden silences, squeezing of my hand, then starting up again as far as her strength would allow.

No, this wasn't what I had feared. This was neither defiance nor stratagem but something much worse, a revelation. Pratap—she could tell me now, couldn't she, now that I wasn't prejudiced against him anymore—Pratap was very complicated, wasn't he? You could think of him in several ways, like anyone else, the successful lawyer, the boy next door. She saw him for what he was after all: a little too young for her, a little too rich, from a set really too different from our own—and these Thakurs, so bigoted, so clannish! Not very clever or handsome, this Pratap, rather lost, being an only child, and his mother dying so early. Really, a very ordinary man with a lot of money, which could serve us well in the future. I knew his money meant security for Madhulika, but more than that, he was her man, secured late in life, still hers alone.

"It took me two years to find out; two years and the threat of losing him when Thakur Sahib tried to marry him off elsewhere [news to me and, I noted, no mention of the imagined pregnancy, that they decided to get married at once]. Oh, I know how much it hurt you all; it hurt me too that you should be hurt, disturbed. But, Chchanda, when he finally married me, it seemed like a miracle!"

She stopped to catch her breath for a minute or two, her hand still lying in the hand of this understanding child with whom she could at last chatter girlishly. "And now see what kind of a miracle it was? How love repaid him?"

This time I put my finger to my lips. I knew someone else who was being repaid pretty well too, someone else who watched her disfigured aunt lying before her, so harmless and somehow so intact, that she sat perfectly still, watching goodness with a kind of stubborn envy, with a sense of being so insignificant, so disarmed in comparison with her

aunt that once Madhu had dozed off, she crept away to
Paro's old room, now Pratap's, and muffling her face in his
bathrobe, wept for no reason and so many reasons that she
feared she would go mad.

By Friday Pratap had managed to become his own master
again, though he insisted on silence to avoid all danger of
a quarrel and planted himself deliberately in the midst of his
bigamy, in which I was assigned the rank of Favorite, the
title of First Wife remaining where it belonged by right.

My presence was no longer indispensable at Panditji's
House and I left with Pratap that morning, in due form
advised by my boss, "Now this time, Chchanda, there's
work to be done." We left an hour earlier, in case we
should, by any chance, waste time before getting down to
work on the files that were waiting for us, especially the
most important of all: "Paradeep Docks versus Pacific Mining Industries."

It was a good system but you had to keep an eye on it
or it had a tendency to get away from you, this over-
discipline, and with no good intentions, I tried to help it
along, holding up my wristwatch from time to time: "Look
Pratap, it's twenty past eleven already."

I don't think he saw any malice in my words, and by
one-thirty he was dictating with all his heart, incidentally
regretting I couldn't take shorthand (what about lunch?)
and I was soon typing, as fast as my rather numb forefingers
could manage, an excellent judicial analysis of the case.
Proud of his work at least, I couldn't help thinking bitterly,

How easy it is to be a man! Love doesn't bother them, doesn't even leave a mark or disturb their capacities. We give in to them, we create impossible situations, turn the world upside-down and ourselves inside-out, they only have to get out of bed to find themselves just where they left off, and the precious career sets them on the track again, as if nothing had happened.

But destiny must have decreed that Pratap's career should suffer a little at least. After about six hours of work, we were beginning to get things really cleared away when the telephone rang. It was the toll exchange from Netarhat and Mala told us Madhulika had suffered a syncope.

You can imagine what Saturday was like. Although Dr. Bose had been able to revive Madhulika quite rapidly, he had been painfully explicit. "Her heart is exhausted, her kidneys are in a terrible state, and the cortisone is having scarcely any effect anymore. From now on it's in God's hands . . . you understand, Chchanda, in God's hands. . . ."

As for the doctor Pratap brought in from Ranchi (I forget his name; in my mind he is Dr. Travel), he expressed himself scarcely less pessimistically, finally allowing us to understand, through a network of circumlocutions and euphemisms, that my aunt's condition was not so much an alert on the part of her system as an admission of failure, and that from now on we would have to be satisfied if we could manage to postpone the end from day to day. Terrified as we were, though less perhaps than at the first great crisis, we went on hoping just the same. A family panics at first, defies the doctors who try to be reassuring; at the end they cling to their hopes and believe even less in the counsels of despair. Madhulika had already survived several attacks in the course of the past few months and the progress of the disease wasn't as spectacular as it had been at the beginning. A darker color in the skin, where the lupus left her enough skin to have any color, a gravelly sound in her voice, a strange retarded quality in her gestures, and a look showing too much white when her eyes moved, were all we could see that indicated much change in our aunt. Our eyes were full of optimism.

She didn't seem to notice much herself and the fact that all of us were at home passed without comment. She was delighted with Pratap's ardor and forgave him for his long hours away, forgave him for leaving her room whenever I entered it. He feared being obliged to pay too much attention to her in front of me; that he need not have feared. And perhaps too of giving himself away: nothing wears away the patience of an old love so fast as a new one. And I tried to encourage him by staying away myself from time to time, leaving Pratap with an opportunity to show himself all the more attentive, and even Paro agreed to the role of the third partner, as adept as either of us in our loving little game.

Of course we were all playing over our heads. I knew how much it cost to maintain our family tableau—every bit of Paro's exasperated efforts, of Pratap's inadmissible patience, not to mention the feelings of one heart-wrung niece.

God knows how we managed to smile at each other and comfort Mala at the same time. And by evening the truce was all but broken when Paro suddenly whispered to me that I should speak to Madhulika about her will.

"Her will?"

"What if she leaves everything to him?"

In spite of my feelings for the old house, for Paro, I decided to speak to Pratap first and he flatly refused to let me bring up any such topic with Madhulika. He told Parvati, "No, Mrs. Horo, I refuse to let my wife be frightened by such things." Paro retreated as if from the lair of a monster, but didn't insist. An hour later, it was obvious she was not emerging from the small room downstairs she had assigned to herself.

"Chchanda," said Pratap, "you will have to get the dinner." And I did in a manner of speaking. But Mala, as aware of the drama as I would have expected her to be, refused to eat. "Go to bed, then," ordered Pratap, and she did.

I hadn't been out of the house since the night before. I ran out for a moment to be alone, to breathe the air in which, along with the smell of the mud, and the sound of the trees, her laughter and the music of her calls had always been dissolved. Under a sky moth-eaten by the first stars, a few reddish clouds prolonged the twilight. I turned to ask the house—something. It was an old trick of mine to give it a face, transforming the door into a mouth, the windows into eyes, the cracks into wrinkles; the time, the season, the play of shadows, the way I felt even gave it the changing expressions I had come to expect. The house was serious now, the trees around it lugubrious and stiff. Two bats fluttered in the air above it, pretending to be mainas on their soft skin wings. I tried to walk down to the Koel, where bits of light still glowed between the black, leaden branches from Thakur Sahib's side of the river. But I quickly drew back, frightened by the sudden hostility of the shadows and especially by the unaccustomed perplexity of my steps. I didn't seem to be walking on my own legs, with my old dancing ease, balancing from one knee to the other as a young girl does. My steps were those of a woman now, more regular, more controlled, careful not to expose myself, to protect the broken wings of a secret fan. It was the kind of walk that didn't lead that way, down to the river.

And I slowly returned to the house where Pratap had switched on just one lamp. He would understand what had drawn me outside, the reasons for my search, would have the right words, the sympathetic gestures. But as if paralyzed by a kind of shy sadness, he could only say, "She's asleep now. I think she's a little better. She's still young, she has the strength to fight." And then, almost whispering, "Go to bed now, my dearest."

And I went upstairs, obedient, resigned. It was just as well, in such circumstances, that our love should call a halt, be postponed, forbidden, like festivities during Ramzan, as if trying to find an excuse for existing. Pratap was right—we should close our eyes, be silent, not think, not imagine, not even foresee. It was right that even at such an hour my seducer, ravaged by his belated delicacy, should send me upstairs alone. Hope itself had become a monstrous thing and lay across the future like a trap. If you don't divorce the aunt to marry the niece, is it any easier, when the aunt dies, to tell the already orphaned niece that you've been speculating on precisely that grisly occurrence? There are some conclusions that murder all beginnings forever afterwards.

Paro was on the landing, waiting for me at Madhulika's door, her eye frozen on Madhulika, who was lying asleep in the purple glow of the nightlight. "Go to bed," she whispered, "I'll stay with her now. If she changes her mind . . ." Paro hesitated, as if such things scarcely concerned me anymore. Then she suddenly took me in her arms, overwhelmed. "Chchanda, I've told her, I made her understand, and you know what she said? 'I'm not dying intestate. And in any case my husband will look after you, Chchanda, and Mala.' Tomorrow, I beg of you, Chchanda, try to make her will over the house to you girls. . . ."

"I'll try," I said, betrayed by pity. And I went into my room. Everything within me cried out in the exalted pride that my aunt had inspired in me. How we deceive ourselves, how different people are from what they seem to be: what depths the surface conceals! Redeeming all her trivialities, her pouts, her faces, her superficial brittle manners, here in extremes, this woman could achieve, could reveal, her true character at last, her faith, in whom? to what? wrapping her corpse in the shroud of her last futile trust, that her charges would not be wronged by the man she loved. At no other moment in life, even when she was so beautiful, so tender and all our own, had I felt so close to my aunt. And I thought: If this is love, what I feel is not. My faithlessness and mistrust were somehow connected with my love for her: If she was absolved, I must be condemned.

Chapter 17

Sunday. I came home from the bazaar in the village square.
Paro wanted vegetables. I went without being noticed, without even noticing who ignored me. A lot of the tribal
Christian population were in the marketplace, shopping for
lunch before they went to the nine o'clock mass. The German ladies, Misses Eba and Elke, were also there, buying
masses of cabbages, which they would make into coleslaw.
The long, strong light already warmed the season's first
flies, rising in the sunbeams: it would be hot weather soon.
The spiders went without their meals, the sundry Chotanagpur birds guzzled their prey in the upper air where the
chimes from the bells of the Roman Catholic church and the
Lutheran church, and the cacophony of the Shiv and Kali
temples, rose like a sonic wave. The woods and the village
were a mass of voices, vendors, songs, cries, even a cuckoo
striking the hour every fifteen minutes or so like a broken
clock. A loudspeaker from a faraway marriage pandal
wafted, "*Hum tum–, ek kamre men bandh ho, aur chabi kho*

jai . . ." Everywhere the wild hibiscus hedges sought forgiveness for their dry winter sulkiness, the japonica for their thorns, by offering, instead, new green leaves in contrast to the pale faded pink—the sickly red flowers falling off their stems apologetically. And the air was filled with an explosive mixture of smells, the cloying smell of the mohua liquor in leaf baskets, the sour smell of the rice beer in large earthen pots, ripened jackfruit and neem-oil smell; only a country nose could pick out what came from the bazaar and what came from the river and the farms, the water hyacinths on the banks and the warm smell from the calf shaking the dried dung from her tail and licking up great mouthfuls of oil cake porridge.

As I reached Panditji's House, the gate creaked and Paro came out, all tricked out in her white sari and blue border, ready for church. "Madhu has no fever now," she said, "but she feels terrible—she's like a rag. Don't leave her alone, and try to keep the other one out of her room. God knows what kind of influence he has."

She hurried on down the road to the center of the village. I knew her routine. She would first call on Rev. Father Monfrais, asking forgiveness for being so happy amongst pagans. Then she and the Rev. Father would have to hurry because this preliminary visit would not leave them much time before Mass. Pratap had repeatedly offered her the car to save her time and her legs, but she had just as repeatedly refused, grumbling behind his back, "Let that infidel drive me to Mass . . . Marcus . . . I'd rather go on my knees!" until

Pratap, taking refuge in discretion, had stopped offering, giving Paro still another excuse for taking offense: "You see, he can't stand Christians! He's an upper-caste Hindu: I can cook for him, but when I go to church, I have to walk!"

I turned to watch her disappear, lifting her starched sari over puddles, but she didn't turn around to look back, and her hard bun and bony figure disappeared behind the grove of frangipani that shielded us from the north. I walked sullenly into the house, putting down my bag of shopping in the kitchen without unpacking or putting things away. Paro could do that after she had prayed for us.

Pratap was in the yellow room sitting on the bed near the pillow. He got up at once, torn between two smiles, one for Madhulika, one for me, his expression ambiguous, as if he were suffering some sudden and absolute necessity. His voice struggled to sound convincing when he said, "Here is Chchanda. Now, my dear, is it all right if I go and get some breakfast?"

"Of course, Pratap," said my aunt, without asking me if I had had mine.

Pratap glided out like a shadow and I sat in his place, where the lightweight yellow quilt was still warm.

"Are you all right, Chchanda?" whispered my aunt.

"First," answered the above-mentioned Chchanda, on a sudden tack of false gaiety, "first of all, we must find out about Mrs. Singh . . . how . . ."

"Oh me! What does it matter now?"

I could have killed Paro. She couldn't leave Madhu alone,

couldn't let her die in peace, still hoping for some miraculous, last-minute change of heart, a last-minute show of a lack of faith in her new husband. But Madhu didn't fool me after all. Corresponding to my false gaiety came this false resignation, this submission eager for the protests it deserved, the assurances that would reawaken hope.

Then came the inevitable commentary, "Poor Pratap, how lonely he'll be when I am gone!"

"Go on, Madhulika! You know he is dying to become a widower—only he's afraid it's going to take years and years!" It's all in the tone. Sometimes the funniest remarks are really the most terrible truths, but somehow made harmless, incredible, contradictory by the way you say them. And Madhu even smiled at my little joke, murmuring, "You never can tell. . . ."

Enough. Stop now before the weight of the words does the rest and gives them their real meaning. With Madhulika in her present state no cunning in the world could take her in for long except a well-rehearsed serenity, a calm that would seem sufficiently self-assured to quieten all her suspicions. So I sat there, next to her, and took up my endless knitting. I satisfied myself by saying what a lovely day it was; cloudy but white.

"Yes," said my aunt, "it is a whitish bright." She seemed to be dozing.

Knit two, purl two, cast off. "Shall I draw the curtains?"

"Yes," said Madhu. She sounded rather faint and lay almost motionless, the sheet under her stretching unwrin-

DAUGHTERS OF THE HOUSE

kled. I began knitting for all I was worth.

It was growing late. Mala was out on one of her rambles, Paro not back from church. I started to worry about lunch. Pratap had looked in twice, both times his wife seemed asleep.

Madhu moved her lips, "I'm thirsty," and then, as I was reaching out for the pot of tepid glucose water, "No, something hot."

I went downstairs. The kitchen was empty but the sound of a match being lit drew Pratap from the living room to where I was standing in front of the gas-stove. "Should I go upstairs?" he asked.

It was almost two days since he had touched me. His resistance was weakening and his eyes were troubled. After all, without going too far, we could certainly kiss each other, could certainly stand there without moving in each other's arms, while the water came to a boil. The bluish flame of the gas trembled under the saucepan, and the first bubbles had not yet appeared. Pratap's hands took liberties and I leaned back a little. The water was boiling now, but I didn't straighten up. Pratap whispered, "Chchanda, Madhuchchanda!"

But suddenly he let me go, almost pushing me away. There was the sound of flapping slippers, and the door to the garden was suddenly pushed open. There stood Paro, breathless, staring at us, finally snapping out, with an oddly unspecified indignation, "You're *both* here!"

I should have explained something, but I was afraid my

voice would tremble; I tried to think how to hide my confusion. Had she seen us through the windows, which, thank God, were filled with bad old glass, or patched with sacking or plywood? If Paro had seen anything, she had learned everything. I was not the kind of niece that leaned in puppyish affection against uncles. Leaning over the saucepan, I began to throw fistfuls of tea leaves into the water. Paro turned right round and sped upstairs.

"She didn't see. . . ." murmured Pratap. He never learned the difference between what Paro didn't see and didn't say. Like all peasant women, she shouted over nothing and fell into long silences over the important.

The infusion of the tea was too strong for Madhu: I started to dilute it, and Mala walked in with some long-stemmed forest flowers. I would have to heat the tea again, strain it . . . what was that?

"Did you hear something?" Pratap asked.

I heard something. Something I understood so well that I rushed upstairs wildly, suddenly beside myself. The sound, the cry, rose, became the high of near-physical pain. The sound grew louder, penetrated the whole house, while Pratap jostled past me to go first into the room, where Paro's hard, long body lay over Madhulika's on the bed. As we came in, she turned on Pratap, her eyes full of tears that magnified her hatred, "There were two of you here, two of you, and you left her alone. . . ." The words collapsed in her throat, she gave up trying to speak and instead started to fold and refold her handkerchief, carefully, slowly, in a certain way.

Madhu was perfectly still but her mask of pustules had suddenly lost its color. And her mouth was open. "There's no pulse," said Pratap. "Get Dr. Bose, get Dr. Bose."

Mala started to cry openly, stepping all over the flowers she had picked. She grabbed one of my wrists. Pratap the other. In a daze we watched Paro tie up Madhulika's chin in her handkerchief and knot it behind her head, as if Madhu had a toothache and was obediently letting Paro look after her. There was a sense of *déjà vu* about the whole scene: we had let Paro look after our ills all our lives. I was a pillar of ice in the heat of March. "Has her heart stopped beating?" asked Mala of no one in particular.

Whose heart had stopped beating, hers or ours? There were two of us in the house, two of us, and we had let her go alone.

Chapter 18

It is hard to imagine just what it is that death deprives you of before it occurs, and even afterwards: a corpse is still there, it is still somehow flesh around what will soon be mere ashes, and seems actually asleep, which is, for us, its last illusion.

I could not entirely believe that Madhulika had died until they took her away at four o'clock in the afternoon. Until that moment, I had merely been an automaton: Misses Elke and Eba came, it seemed, within minutes. They asked for Madhulika's favorite set of clothes, a grey and pink chiffon outfit, no, no shoes, eau de cologne, but she loved Ma Griffe's "Carven," all right then, let's have that. I cleaned up the room, took away the medicine bottles, received the visitors, of which there were many. Madhulika was not only the daughter of Panditji's House, she was also Thakur Sahib's daughter-in-law. We did not have a family pandit, being Brahmins ourselves, nor were we given to any formal practice of religion. But Thakur Sahib brought along one from Ranchi with him at around two in the afternoon. The pandit asked us to put Madhulika on the floor; Pratap, Thakur Sahib, Paro, and I all refused. The pandit let it pass; he was too much in awe of Thakur Sahib. I took part in all those distractions that nevertheless manage to occupy grief: the death certificate, sandalwood, notifications. I watched the tradesmen bow in their purchased compassion as they ran hither and thither collecting ghee, wood, bamboo, and flowers. And I added up the cost, since you (or Thakur Sahib) had to pay for this mourning; he who wouldn't pay for the wedding. I was scarcely conscious of what I was doing the whole time; it was as if I were anesthetized by an affliction that, taken in too strong a dose, had become its own painkiller.

My courage failed me when they actually started to take her out of the house—Pratap, Thakur Sahib, Dr. Bose, and Mr. Prabhakar, for whose wife I remember sewing and embroidering all my young life, until good times in the form of Pratap came upon us. Mala stood on the landing and suddenly started to throw up. I backed towards the front door. Paro screamed: "Pratap! Take the girls away, be good for something!" Everyone was taken aback, mostly Thakur Sahib, who had never imagined any servant could scream at his son thus. But Paro was an acknowledged "character" in these parts, and all put it down to hysteria. Anyway, Pratap was bearing the pall and could do nothing. I took Mala to our bathroom, cleaned and changed her, put a drop of aquapsycotis in a glass of water for her, and dragged her by the hand into the woods, all the time thinking, Paro will never forgive Pratap; she has said nothing except for the *faux pas* of minutes ago, respecting the truce that even the greediest legatees abide by for as long as the body is in the house. But it was all the more on her mind.

She held Pratap triply responsible. By marrying my aunt he had broken up the existence that had suited us so well. By marrying her at that age in life, he had caused her to fall ill of the dread disease. As a matter of fact, tuberculosis of all kinds was quite rampant in our region. He had prevented her from making such a will as would leave everything to her nieces. And lastly he had tempted her niece from her bedside, when perhaps a final needle with a dose of something may have saved her for a few hours; Rev. Father Monfrais could have come. Or, all right, even a pandit or Dr. Markham. One ought not to die without someone religious nearby. And all alone. I remembered as if it was a thousand years ago, Pratap saying, "Shall I go up to her?" And try as I would, I couldn't avoid thinking: Now, she knows!

In the woods, I looked at the trees. I knew the ones planted in the year of my own mother's birth by Panditji and those planted in the year of Madhulika's birth. Branch by branch they had witnessed her growth, had accompanied her in life, and now, despite their knots and gnarls, had survived her death. I saw the delight of the sparrows flying with twigs in their beaks, a little too early for home building and the crazy exhibitionism of a squirrel turning what looked like cartwheels. None of it seemed out of place. Panditji's daughters had not loved his house as much as his granddaughter did—the house would not mourn for Madhulika.

They returned from the burning ghat at eight in the evening. Wagner clumsily patted my head, "Remember, Chchanda, it is a deliverance for her. . . ." A deliverance. Yes, I remembered. And I knew that it was no less one for him; that he had come purposely to remind his precious son, for whom also it was . . . a deliverance.

"Let me drop you off on the way," said Thakur Sahib to Dr. Markham and his sisters. They left; so did Dr. Bose, and the others followed.

All this while Paro was in the kitchen, loudly reciting a Latin requiem in Adivasi accents, which she knew by rote. It sounded like "Dem Mary, Pula prrie, dis boom Jesus, when the rose is called the painoo I'll be dere." After everyone had left, she came to me and asked in a stage whisper, "When is he leaving? Did he say anything about leaving tomorrow?"

"Who?"

"Pratap. He can't stay here anymore. There are young girls in the house!"

A classic case of locking the stable doors after the horse had been stolen, I thought, and started to cry bitterly on Paro's shoulder.

The truce was broken the very next day; the relationships she left behind began to cool even more quickly than the ashes of my aunt's funeral pyre. Where there had formerly been nothing more than dismay, now bitterness, though always disguised, began to make itself felt. The battle-lines were drawn up: always under the cover of propriety. In a matter of a few hours, Panditji's House was nothing more than the lists where Pratap and Paro confronted one another, underhandedly, careful to admit nothing of their real feelings, their real purposes, relying instead on the mean and endless questions of legality.

Pratap sat behind his plate of boiled potatoes and vegetables (grief must go hungry if it is genuine). There was white cheese which we all hated, to go with it. He began, "Mrs. Horo, do you happen to have Mr. Kiron Mukherjee's address? I don't have it, and of course he must be written to."

"It's taken care of. He is with the Ramakrishna Mission in Calcutta's Golpark. I've already posted a letter to him." The fact of my father's existence was news to me.

"Good," said Pratap, but his brows drew together. He went upstairs.

"Paro," I asked in wonder, "how did you know where my father was?"

"Well, he sent some checks after your mother died and when I threw him out. He wrote again after Madhu's marriage, but as long as you two were in Madhu's charge, he was sanguine it would be all right. You, Chchanda, have almost ten months left before you cease to be a minor. In the meantime, you must have a guardian appointed, not that one! Kiron has wandered around a lot, but now he is with the mission. A rolling stone, that one. Hope he will be of some use to us now. . . . Listen! What is that Pratap doing? He is putting his things back into Madhu's room!" She looked hard at me as if I were somehow to blame, or at least I could account for what Pratap was doing. Her chin began to tremble: uncertainty, along with her will to respect this day, as well as the presence of Mala, prevented her from screaming at me, "But what does he want here now? What is he doing in our house, anyway? His wife is dead, our baby. Now he should have the decency to leave!"

I understood very well what she meant without her having to say a word. With Mala at my heels, I went upstairs in my turn. Paro followed me, smiling and saying loud enough to carry, "You know, Chchanda, I wanted to keep everything just the way it was in her room." In the yellow room, I suddenly felt a pang that almost doubled me up in pain. The bed had been neatly made, the sheets drawn up smoothly under the canary yellow quilted bedcover. Pratap was rummaging in the wardrobe. "Don't bother, Mr. Singh," said Paro sweetly, "I'll take care of all that in the next few days."

Pratap didn't answer, but turned his eyes towards me, seeking an answering glance, an ally.

"You're going to sleep here now?" I asked, almost whispering.

"Where else could I sleep? Mrs. Horo must have her room back."

Exasperated by my neutrality, he began putting papers

back in the open wardrobe, taking others out. I recognized them all—the piles of bills, letters, coupons—it was my aunt's touching disorder, signifying futility at best. She spent money only on good clothes, very few of them but of the very best quality, good makeup, and one jar of perfume at a time. She must have subconsciously considered these things a form of investment.

I was thinking up a sentence that would make both Paro and Pratap understand that neither of them had a right to a demonstration of authority here, when Pratap took the lead. "I'm sorry to speak of such things to you children. You can't imagine how complicated such things can become. You are both minors. . . ."

All spoken so mildly, so benevolently, without suspecting for an instant, the sudden wave of hostility that rushed through me, burning my throat. Minor! I was also a minor on the twenty-fourth of March and it didn't seem to bother him then! Today was only the first of April.

Yet, he continued in the same tone: "And two minor daughters with a father alive, who, of course, might wish to resume his rights, a board of guardians rather difficult to determine, since there are no close relations, and a legacy that consists entirely of this house, and is therefore indivisible estate, not to mention the interminable legal formalities . . . well, there are some hard days ahead, I fear."

"You are complicating things," said Paro, "each girl has her half of Panditji's House. All they have to do is to stay together as they have always done, and that's that!"

Pratap turned towards her. Both had dropped their casual manner and I listened to them with distaste. "Don't deceive yourself, Mrs. Horo. It is true that Madhulika cannot will away her father's house from her nieces, who are his granddaughters. They are now the joint owners of it. But there is no way in which they could maintain it without the interest of Madhu's meager fixed deposits, which now belong to me. Of course, I will gladly relinquish . . ."

"The deposits . . . Holy Mother of God . . ." stammered Paro, furious and dazed.

"Don't worry about it now," said Pratap. "I'll take care of it. It will all turn out for the best."

He looked at me again, seeking my eyes and my approval, and found neither. I was frightened. Why hadn't I thought of this? Even the little legal knowledge I had acquired in Pratap's office let me know that husbands and wives usually made out their fixed deposit receipts jointly, either or survivor. Pratap had us in his power now. He was paying for the running of this house and had every right to be in this room. We were the sudden slaves of his generosity, so that, if by any chance I did not show myself to be properly grateful, he could force me to sell the house. My house! Panditji's House. Paro was watching me, certain of my reaction, but at least I had wits enough not to betray myself to either of them. Caution! Prudence! Care! I had Pratap in my power too. A properly languishing smile would recompense him for his generosity.

And then I murmured with the right touch of innocence

and distress, "Listen, Pratap, all this is very embarrassing and confusing. But I want you to know right away that I will never, never forgive anyone who makes me give up this house. It means more to me than anyone or anything in the world." The words were tough and uncompromising; the tone ready to realize that I could be speaking in a moment of great distress and was therefore susceptible to advice; the whole scene redolent of the parting scenes in Hindi movies with strains of *"Babul mora naihar choot hi jai"* in the imaginary background.

Neither Pratap nor Paro was satisfied. Pratap would have liked me to say, "It makes no difference, I am going to marry Pratap anyway; as for you, Paro, you are only the cook here!"

Paro would have liked me to yell: "Your wife is dead, now get out! We have managed before; we'll manage again."

Both realized I couldn't bear any more; that I was incapable of listening to either of them in front of that canary yellow bedspread. Paro quietly left. Pratap drew me close to him and said, "My poor darling, we'll sort it out." I tolerated his kiss. But as I walked away towards my own room I unconsciously wiped it off with my sleeve.

Once in my room, in spite of exhaustion, in spite of wanting to be merely a girl who has lost her aunt, her *de facto* mother, and who gives way to her grief, I began to walk back and forth in my bare feet. No footwear for four days, the pandit decreed.

What was happening? As far as Panditji's House was concerned, the situation was serious enough. But that wasn't all. Never had I understood my own motives less clearly. Between Pratap and me, suddenly, there was a barrier of fire. It was no use telling myself that his tactics were obvious. Panditji's House was his enemy where I was held captive. It was a financial burden to which were added Mala and Paro. A good sale for which he could scarcely be held responsible, which insurmountable legal and financial difficulties might force on us, would serve his purpose nicely. And once Panditji's House was sold off, there could be no reason for Mrs. Horo to hang on. Pension her off. Mala's share of the sale money would give her the excellent education she deserved. He would have only me to deal with then. It was all so easy: Just play the obvious variations on the same simple theme; no more Panditji's House, no more Chchanda.

But it wasn't so easy. Our small dispute was scarcely important enough to account for my uneasiness, or to justify this rejection, this withdrawal from Pratap that I suddenly started to feel. My eagerness to surrender myself to my grief—dirtied, poisoned as it was by my own unworthiness—was nearer the truth, and Pratap himself must have known it better than I, for he scarcely dared brush against me or look me in the eye, and bided his time until some less critical hour, contenting himself with the role of widower-uncle. But there was something else, too, something that made our separation even deeper. It spread between us like a trench—I stopped. No not a trench, a grave. Again the same thought flashed through my mind, She knows, now she knows.

And from where she was, wouldn't she know something else, too? Couldn't she see that there would never be anything between Pratap and me again? You can't make an accomplice into a comrade, and when your own happiness is based on your aunt's happiness or misery, an aunt who is all the mother you have ever known, how can you profit by her death without considering your joy a crime? Dying, but still alive, Madhulika had brought us together; dead at last, she divided us forever. There are no divorces granted from the grave. I could steal my aunt's husband from her but not her widower. Perhaps Pratap had his own reasons too, for getting rid of Panditji's House. Would he dare sleep with you on that primrose-colored bed? You have to choose one or the other; one and not the other. And how can you live anywhere but here? Your choice is already made. Of the two punishments, you have certainly chosen the lighter.

The house had somehow avenged itself now on the man who had smuggled himself under its roof by banishing him forever. Could the man avenge himself in turn? How? By forcing us to sell. Paro's writing to my father wouldn't be enough. I would have to write too. Gather forces. Above all, somehow, get together quite a lot of money.

Half an hour later, I read over the letter. What feelings would this unknown father have for us after our mother's tragic death so many years ago? He had abandoned us to

Madhulika and Paro, never tried to see us. We were scarcely aware that he was alive; sometimes a little money came for us and once, that box of dates. From what I had heard of him, he would probably be distressed by the amount of paperwork it would involve him in, asking the court to make Paro my guardian for the next few months. I was aware of Kiron Mukherjee's remoteness from us even as I stamped the envelope.

Pratap was still rummaging upstairs. Madhulika must have forgotten to tell him where the family papers were kept. Forgotten or neglected to?

I had an inspiration and leapt up; something I remembered from childhood. In the sitting room, the fourth telephone directory, year 1950. The heavy book slid open. It was hollowed and offered me lots of old papers and two surprises: one good, one bad. There was a small tin box from Flury's, red and gold—inside it was what my grandmother used to call her "mop-chain," a thick gold rope that fell from the neck to the feet. It was supposed to be worn in several loops. Despite our perennial family decay, my grandmother had saved that. The other thing I found was a new envelope. Inside, on a piece of paper, were these extravagant lines: "I the undersigned, Madhulika Singh, née Chakravorty, bequeath to my husband, Pratap Singh, all the disposable share of my property, and to the degree that their father, my brother-in-law, Kiron Mukherjee, will consent, name Pratap Singh the guardian of my nieces, Madhuchchanda and Mala Mukherjee. I also bequeath to my husband one third of my paternal house, in these parts known as Panditji's House. It is a freehold property. . . ."

Thank God I had come in time! Pratap may know the law, but he knew nothing about Madhulika having made a will.

Chapter 19

I have never been able to decide whether I should be proud or ashamed of what followed. Whatever we do, I suppose the best of it cancels out the worst, and we scarcely know the value of the result—perhaps it would be impossible to live if we had to know the value exactly. You think you're behaving unselfishly, making heroic sacrifices, and then it turns out that the "sacrifice" is really a kind of brutal pleasure for some secret place of yourself. You think you're being worthlessly egoistic, and suddenly you see you've exercised your selfishness so weakly that everyone except yourself has taken advantage of it. Dupes, first and foremost, that's what we are, dupes. . . .

And at Panditji's House it was only a question of degree: Who was the more deceived and who the less?

I had hoped to be up first the next morning but Paro was already downstairs with Pratap arguing about lawyers. She held out for our own Mr. Mitra; Pratap was for his Mr. Roy, pointing out that in case my father wrote and preferred not

to use Mr. Mitra, Mr. Roy could still be retained to represent the other party's interests. I kept out of the argument,
and since Pratap himself seemed anxious not to involve me,
I let him leave the house around nine o'clock to consult the
lawyer of his own choosing.

Paro turned on me at once. "What a thirty-six hours!
She's out there, her ashes cast into the Koel, and he's still
around. . . ." Luckily she stopped there, busying herself
with things to do in the kitchen.

That evening, when Pratap returned with Mr. Roy to do
the first estimates, I understood why she had not left me
alone for a second the whole day. Mr. Roy was given tea,
and when he asked where Mrs. Singh usually kept her
papers, Paro led him to the yellow room, where in a catch-
drawer of Madhulika's dressing-table, where "Madhu kept
her papers," we discovered two rings of little value and a
fixed deposit receipt of seventy thousand rupees, valid for
three years at 10 percent interest in the names of Parvati
Horo, Madhuchchanda Mukherjee, and Mala Mukherjee;
583 rupees per month. The receipt was certainly not there
the day before.

During the following few days, Paro, assuming she had
me well in hand again, made no difficulties about my going
back to work in Ranchi. She even whispered, "I don't like
you going back there, but the other one gets round the law
like a water-fowl on the Koel and it's good for you to keep
an eye on what he's doing."

But I didn't know what I was doing myself. Pratap rather

frightened me these days—and his self-assurance, easily equal to Paro's—impressed me. With the blindness of a man in love, he counted on me: a woman in love will do anything; a house with the key in your pocket. He did not want the house, did not want the key, all he wanted was me, away from the house and its influence.

The very next day, not to be outdone by his adversary (he knew where the fixed deposit receipts suddenly came from), Pratap went to Mr. Roy's office, and in my presence, almost carelessly renounced all claim to Madhulika's money that was in their joint names, making the total of our reserves, a lakh and fifty thousand, enough for Paro, Mala, and myself to live in genteel comfort for the rest of our lives. This action of Pratap's moved me more than I thought it could and he emphasized its effect by surrounding me with all the discreet attentions of a beloved.

But an unexpected visit from Wagner, who shut himself in the office with his son for an hour, ruined everything. The mere presence of this man, actually a morganatic grand-uncle, in the private office of my uncle-in-law, cruelly under-lined the ambiguity of the situation. The visit undoubtedly signified that Thakur Sahib had pardoned his son and heir for the blunder from which a merciful destiny had liberated him, and in a fever of paternal solicitude had come to urge his offspring that the two nieces of his wife were hardly his responsibility. Just exactly what Paro wanted. The idea that he suspected me of hanging on to Pratap for what I could get out of him made me bristle, but did me good. It was one argument more if I wanted out. But an argument that became untenable when, after two or three loud outbursts, Wagner rushed out of the office. Had Pratap, anticipating what he felt sure would be my consent, been foolish enough to let him suspect something? Did that angry glare accuse me of having taken after my aunt and cast my net over his heir across the river?

My confusion must have warned Pratap, who interpreted it the wrong way around, closed the door, and threw his arms around me. "Don't worry, Chchanda. My father wanted me to stay here in Ranchi and of course I couldn't tell him, at least not right now. . . ."

Inside me I screamed, Listen to the old man. Stay here or go to hell. We have Paro's money and Madhu's, which you made over to us, morally ours anyway, and you know nothing about the will, so the house is ours too.

He leaned over me, but I turned my head away, shaking my straight, uncompromising hair between us.

The real accounting didn't take place until the end of the week. At our house as well as in the office, Pratap began to get fidgety. He found it harder and harder to take Paro's poisonous remarks without answering back. With me he tried to return to a state of prenuptial tenderness, tinged with compassion, but carried it off badly. My own reluctance to make any concessions at all, he had undoubtedly explained to himself as distress, an anguished, somewhat delayed act of penitence towards the dead. Perhaps, too, he interpreted it as a postponed reaction of delicacy, the ideal of a spoiled passion that suddenly catches a glimpse of its own possibilities and therefore suspends its provisional gifts in order to make itself worthy of its definitive bestowal, to re-create its own virginity. The upper-class Indian male mind is capable of anything, any conceit.

In the end, though, he couldn't stand any more of it, and when we reached the office, he clasped me in his arms without warning. I struggled like a wet slab of soap but he was everywhere. "Chchanda, I know what you are thinking. You are thinking you were my mistress, because you couldn't be my wife, and now you don't have to be my mistress any longer because I can marry you. And that's all I want, I couldn't ask for anything more. . . ."

He kept my head firmly wedged in the crook of his elbow so that my mouth was full of the material of his safari suit and his skin. "I understand your situation, darling," he went on, "but relax a little. I'm not very happy either, you know. I wasn't made for this sort of thing any more than you. But we're free now . . . I love you."

"Now" was perhaps the one word never to be used to qualify our liberty.

"I love you": the son of Wagner's old argument, played twice on the same record, in the same room. The words rang in my head, recovering all their meaning: now it's our turn to get married, he loves me, doesn't he, after my aunt who had her chance at this same love, and now bequeaths it to me, free and aboveboard, the only part of my inheritance. How could Pratap deceive himself about me to such a degree? Holding me even closer, he began, "Of course people will talk at first. . . ."

And behind his voice and its promises of marriage, I could already hear the dreadful murmurs, the malicious mouth at the ready ear: "Have you heard about it? First the aunt, then the niece—maybe even at the same time!" I could already see Pratap's colleague, Mr. Prasad's, bewilderment—hadn't he said to me before, "Mrs. Singh, I presume?" And now he would have to learn it all over again, "Not Miss Mukherjee, this time it's Mrs. Singh." Even in the mouths and minds of those least inclined to slander, what confusion there would be, both Madhu, both "made legal," thanks to Pratap's speciality of whitewashing dirty walls, to use an old expression of our part of the country, where anything irregular is taken badly and is as quickly torn to shreds by backbiters as a bad job of limewashing can be torn off a wall by sharp nails.

"But I have a few tricks up my sleeve, Chchanda, I'll tell you in a little while. . . ."

All right. In a little while. You have to be nice first, have to give a pledge, you detestable Chchanda. Do it then, one more time, I'll give you permission: one last time for the shame you deserve, for the advantage you can take of him, but not for pleasure. A few tricks? What tricks? You had better find out. Every spy knows that a man tells everything afterwards, everything. . . .

Chapter 20

He told everything. Scarcely freed from an embrace in which I had renounced my own share of pleasure (and discovered how parasitical a man can seem, clinging to us in his silly climax like a misshapen orchid in the crotch of some jungle tree), Pratap recovered his solemn lawyer's manner, as if he were about to take the stand, and as soon as he had straightened his clothes and combed his hair said, "Listen to me, Chchanda. I'm going to speak very frankly. You don't seem to understand that we may be separated any minute. The situation is more serious than you think."

There was nothing particularly dramatic in the way he cleaned out his comb, pulling out the hairs from between rather greasy teeth. Someone had written, some historical personage from Austria, during the beginning of World War II, "The situation is impossible but not serious." My reviving irony, indispensable ally of my reviving hostility, watched Pratap closely, forgetting itself a little in its regrets: I used to like to use that comb to do his parting myself.

"It all depends on you," continued Pratap. "I've written to Kiron Mukherjee, asking him to transfer to me those rights that reverted to him on Madhulika's death. They are rights I have already exercised. [I couldn't forbear smiling.] Either he will or he won't. And in any case, when we get married, the question is closed."

As usual, my silence during moments of crisis—a real collapse—encouraged Pratap. I was still lying inertly on the bed, my clothes crushed under me, the kind of position that implies total consent. Pratap plucked up his courage. "The stumbling block, you know, is Panditji's House. I appreciated your speech about it the other day—a splendid little tirade. But think it over a little more carefully, Chchanda. We're going to find ourselves in a tight spot here. Apart from finances, people are so unkind sometimes. You know what I mean?"

I knew all right. I even managed to nod my head a little, closing my eyes like a cat when she sees a mouse coming. He interpreted my silence, I suppose, as the indifference of a woman entirely possessed by her own passion. He finished up irritably, "Well, let's not mince words! I can't bury myself for life in your precious, tumbledown old house, miles from anywhere, with an old servant who hates me and a younger sister who has to be seen through life. Paro should be pensioned off; the house sold; Mala's share of the money will see her through an excellent education; you and I can give her a home—and yours, my love, your share from the sale of Panditji's House will make you a nice little dowry." (Smiling wolfishly.)

My tender-hearted friend had even thought about my dowry to make up for the losses he had incurred while living with us. "Of course," he continued, "if Paro wants to rent a small place and have Mala live with her in Ranchi, instead of going into the hostel, I don't see anything wrong with that." No, Pratap, it wouldn't make any difference to your program or to your sentence.

Pratap thought his victory was won. His expression that night seemed to say as much when we got back to Panditji's House. A quarrel was inevitable, and we had scarcely entered the front door when Paro, pretending to address me, began, "I looked in at Mr. Mitra's this morning. He wasn't too happy not being consulted. . . ."

Pratap rashly interrupted her, "Mrs. Horo, until informed to the contrary, I am in control of my nieces. I ask you to leave the matter in my hands. If you do not, I shall be forced to do without your services here." As he stammered, his eyes fell at his own impudence.

Mine did too. My dearest old Paro, to be talked to in that manner, so bitterly abused! I had a tart word on my lips already, but of all things, Paro was smiling! Imperturbably, she replied, "It seems to me, Mr. Singh, that we can do without your services here, sooner than mine." There was a peculiar irony in her voice, but Pratap didn't notice it.

Nor could he control himself any longer. "Are you so

foolish as to think that anyone in their right minds will allow these two Brahmin girls to be brought up solely by a Christian tribal servant?"

From the sudden way she threw back her head, I thought the underhanded thrust had gone home, but I was mistaken. Paro's black face looked haughtily at Pratap and, finally, with a look of unspeakable triumph, she said, "We have managed to be secular and self-supporting before you came here and we will manage again. As for your 'anyone in their right minds,' the first thing they will wonder about is why an uncle-in-law should be sticking to these girls so closely, who are nothing to him, and under age."

"What do you mean?" shouted Pratap.

Paro had already turned her back.

Neither of them knew it but I felt sure it was the beginning of the end.

Chapter 21

So many things are determined by chance: a quick shower
that morning had discouraged me from going to the market-
square to do Paro's chores for her. By the time I did go and
return, there wasn't a chance in ten that I would meet the
postman, but there he was, drunken old Kishun, delighted
not to have to make the trip to our house, where Paro never
even offered him a cup of tea, let alone a drink. "Ho,
Chchanda," he yelled, "take the mail for me, will you?"

There was a lot of mail. Many letters of condolence from
Madhu's Brabourne College friends to us, a letter from
Paro's cousin, who was the block development officer at
Ichaghar on the Roro river and who had arranged all her
compensation money so smoothly. And one from Kiron
Mukherjee. "These painful times, the time involved . . .
affection and trust in Madhulika . . . so young to die . . .
regrets he could do nothing for his children . . . was with
the mission, very rewarding work . . . appointed Mrs. Parvati Horo their guardian until they came of age." Not one

word about Pratap. Our long-lost father had saved the day!

I walked a little faster. I wanted to prepare Paro for carrying off her triumph discreetly. Later, I would make Pratap understand that, even if he had lost control of the situation, he hadn't necessarily lost me. Perhaps it would be better if he went away for a little while so as not to compromise me by an unaccustomed insistence that might make our marriage suspect even later on. Actually he didn't want the guardianship at all; he merely wanted a weapon against Panditji's House, his real rival, and if—without actually promising anything—I could make him believe that he had nothing to fear, that in fact his presence was actually spoiling our plans, which his departure would make easier, maybe he would agree to go.

It would be the same suitcase he had come with. How much it had bothered him that day! The executioner of this little ceremony was not exactly blithe, despite her new freedom-to-be, despite the fresh wind that lifted her *dupatta* and chastised the trees around our house that were a little too proud of their young leaves for a house in mourning.

Pratap's car was parked in the onion and potato shed. What the hell was he doing here now? He was striding towards me and I would soon find out. "It can't go on any longer, Chchanda!" He seemed really upset. "Paro was speaking to Mala just now; I had come home unexpectedly and she shouted, 'I have no food for that one!' I don't want to make a scene, but I can't take it anymore."

So go, I thought, but the next moment I was filled with

sorrow and shame. The son of Thakur Sahib, from the house of plenty, taking such treatment and all for my unworthy self!

"You've got to leave with me, Chchanda!"

"To set the whole village talking?"

"You don't have to sleep at my place. There is a woman who runs a boarding house for working girls. You can live there."

What a splendid way to keep up appearances; safe by night, sinning by day.

Paro was already at the door, sticking out her chin as if our conversation were a personal offense. My peace-making mission wouldn't be easy.

"Pratap, I think it would be better if you just stayed by yourself in Ranchi for a while. Better all around."

"No," said Pratap, "no, I can't leave you. This place has too much influence on you, and she . . ."

He must have had antennae. He stood in my path and something bitter in his voice touched me more than I wanted it to. The mail was still under my arm, luckily. Details like this have ruined so many dramas, distracted the attention at just the wrong moment. I went forward with the letters just as Paro came to the front door, shouting: "You heard what he was saying last night, didn't you? How he talked to me? He has a bed in town and one across the river too, doesn't he? Why does he have to dirty our sheets, Marcus!" Her eyes were as hard as glass and even nastier than her words. But suddenly they grew very small and

shiny and cunning between indulgent lids. I had been stut-
tering, "But I was just trying to . . ."

"Try again," hissed Paro, "you can make him do anything."

My chance came right away. Pratap was in the sitting-
room and I wondered at his thick skin. He had thought it
over, he said, and decided I was avoiding him, trying to gain
time. Time, I discovered, was what Pratap needed most of
all. He trapped me against the bookcase, desperate. "Let us
go now, darling, without saying anything. It's the best way.
You can write to her from Ranchi, and I'll come back and
get your things." So the schedule called for abduction.
"Your father won't refuse his consent. We can get married
at the Arya Samaj. Then we can leave for anywhere." His
knee was between my legs, his hands on my breasts: according to his own lights, I suppose he played his cards well and
didn't overlook his best argument, the one that spoke to my
body and out-classed all others. Only it didn't work. "Let's
go now," he repeated, his mouth coming towards mine.

Now, Chchanda, since we have to dot every *i* to let my
guardian angel be sure of what he had suspected from the
very first, since we have to give him a weapon against us
anyway, we'll allow one more kiss, this one the last. Whatever you thought, Pratap, my beloved, I'll remember it
gratefully, although you hurt me more last time—making
plans for us, disposing of Mala and Paro—more than I have
ever been hurt before.

The door was open, and Paro, creeping in on her treacher-ous, institutional Keds, stood watching us with a look of satisfaction on her face. "Get out of here!" she said.

If I had been Pratap, oh, if I had been Pratap, I would have turned and answered right in her face, "I certainly will, Mrs. Horo; in fact, we both will and straightaway. You see, we are in love!"

But Pratap, my jurist, look at him! He had no such ideas. He turned ashen, immediately let me go, and struggled to regain his dignity. He began to quibble, "It's not at all what you think, Mrs. Horo. . . ."

"Get out of here!" Paro repeated.

Pratap could still recover his position—all he had to do was to take me by the wrist and run off with his prey, who had neither the strength nor the wits nor even the will to struggle against him at just that moment and who was choking on the sudden certainty that he could never save her from what she deserved. But instead, Pratap just stood there, stammering, embarrassed by my silence, "Tell her, Chchanda, explain . . . say something."

"Get out of here!" said Paro. She stood stock-still in the doorway, as stubborn as a bulldog whose face alone is enough to frighten away prowlers.

Pratap's hand was on the doorknob. His pallor was rising and falling like a gone-mad thermometer. I could see the anger begin to swell at the back of his neck. Was he going to turn around and break anything? The coy Venus de Milo or the legless shepherd; behave like Lochinvar or throw the blame on me? I was standing there, nailed to the floor, in terror.

No, not even that. He regained control of himself, tossed his head, disappointed, woebegone even, but prudent. Perhaps determined to save his strength for the next round, even managing to cover his retreat. "You were right, Chchanda, I'll go. You know where you can find me."

"I'll put a stop to that," said Paro, finally leaving off her refrain.

For a moment, because it was a moment of wrangling, Pratap found his old manner again. "You have no business interfering in this matter. The girl has her legal rights and you know it as well as I."

"If you know it so well," replied Paro, "I think you also ought to know I represent Kiron Mukherjee here from now on until Chchanda is eighteen and I told you, GET OUT OF HERE."

That explained everything. Paro's magnificent *sangfroid* of last night came straight out of the notary's office. As did Pratap's haste. He must have had a letter from Kiron Mukherjee this morning like myself. Neither of us had mentioned it: Paro, so that I wouldn't leave with Pratap in a burst of resentment, hoping I would tell him to clear out, of my own accord; Pratap, so that he could compromise me to the last, reconciling affection with authority, putting an end to the whole business before my newfound independence began to jib. Surrounded by subterfuges, it was

scarcely the moment for the shouts or screams that tradi-
tionally honor the epilogue of a well-made play. I could still
transfer the victory from one to the other; all I had to do
was to follow Pratap out of that door where he had just
disappeared.

Paro didn't even stand in my way, and as if to encourage
me, slapped my face hard and unexpectedly. "Slut!" she
said. Suddenly, though, she collapsed on a chair, looking at
her hand. I looked at her: every day of service to us was
etched on her face. Its expression had that world sorrow
that you see on the faces of workmen and housewives
when they are eating their food alone. There is no particular
reason for the expression. If hearts could break, mine broke
then. Paro, oh, Paro. But I remained still.

Upstairs we heard objects being moved across the floor,
the noise of the wardrobe doors. Then the stairs creaked
under the footsteps of a man whom two infatuated women
had not been able to teach in over ten months that the sixth
step was broken. Finally, after several false starts—great
screams of the accelerator that filled the silence like calls, as
if in the hope that a sudden passenger would fling herself
out of the door at the last minute—there was the sound of
a car in gear, proclaiming its speed on the nearby road.

"And about time," said Paro.

But in our house, where everyone pays for what they get,
Paro will have to pay for that slap and keep paying for a
long, long time. Just now, my only answer, one that makes
her drop her eyes, is a certain look.

Now we can go upstairs with a sure step: lunch has not been eaten nor will be. We are as determined as we are restrained. Each step lifts me higher than Paro who is following. Mala is with me. I push her into my old room, which I used to share with her. "You can have your old room back, Paro," I say.

As the oldest daughter of the house now, I walk into Madhulika's yellow room and shut the door.

Chapter 22

The inventory. Mine would be so different from Mr. Roy's (had there been one), passing disdainfully through our rooms, little figures at the tip of his tongue. The left side of the wardrobe is empty now—Pratap left only the hangers. The drawer he used is empty too: just a broken watch-strap, which I throw into a wastepaper basket. The smell of Brut is persistent, but we'll air out the room. Some of these old houses in cold places like Ranchi and Netarhat have fire-places; this one has. It is never lit but will be this time. And we'll spare the transistor. Mass-produced items don't make good fetishes. Pratap's photograph goes into the fire. As I watch the picture twist and melt, I decide to replace it with Madhulika's—later, when I wouldn't offend her memory every time I looked at her face. For now, so as not to offend mine, let's sort out her clothes, linen, papers, everything. Pratap did it just the other day. But he didn't know what to look for or, rather, what not to look for. You don't leave love letters for an inheritance. Madhulika must have had those destroyed, along with her powder-puff when it became redundant. Everything less than a year old will have to be destroyed. But so many things are unbearable! Five of the new nightdresses in all their myriad shades of yellow are still in their tissues. All these bottles, tubes, and pots as powerless to save her beauty as all the pharmaceutical glassware had been to save her life. I decided to keep her old red dressing-gown.

One ironclad rule: The souvenirs of Mrs. Singh must go. They were not the souvenirs of Madhulika; we were no longer rivals, having both abandoned the same man. He could scarcely be abandoned or forgotten by one of us without having to eliminate all traces of him from the other's life as well. Pratap had left me no letter, no ring, not one keepsake, and now that I was left as unprovided for as a nun who has lost even her faith, I couldn't bear to live among the idols of another cult.

Already the things made a good-sized bundle on the canary yellow bedspread. "Take down the curtains, Mala," I said. She brought a stool and worked wordlessly. We would use only the oldest tenants of all our chests. My grandmother's linen—twelve lime green sheets with a money-plant leaf embroidered in the corner, twelve towels ditto, six white sheets and pillow-towels, and thirty-six white towels, these we would live with. Not the lovely new stuff that had come in recently. Mala and I tied up the four corners of the bedspread. I walked towards the Koel with the bundle on my shoulders, like a *dhobi*, and dumped the whole lot into the water. The river took it all quickly and everything sank under the humming surface. Had my strength left me just at that moment, had I suddenly known that I was behaving childishly, that my "justice" was wasteful, it wouldn't have mattered anymore. I knew my sacrifice, like all sacrifices, was a punishment in which I sought protection. You can't have everything. If you pay for your joy with shame, you don't recover your pride again without exchanging it with misery.

Mala is wiser than I. To every end there is a beginning and she knows exactly what to say. "Did you see the little sal trees by the river's edge, Chchanda? They are so . . . so fat, even, already."

Madhu will never see the sal trees as they grow, sprout by sprout, assailing the old trunks that I count over and over again. They are contracted to a man in Daltongunj. The river pushes on its way, and if love renounces, Panditji's House remains.

Chapter 23

By the time we returned from the river, Parvati had redone the yellow room. My grandmother's off-white *tussore* curtains were hung up. They were naturally a perfect fit, being meant originally for this room. My clothes were in the wardrobe. A patchwork bedcover was on the bed. The room was not so pretty now but somehow more durable and solid.

Our finances were not in a bad way, either. There was Paro's seventy thousand, plus Madhulika's (and Pratap's) eighty thousand, making a total of a lakh and a half, which meant an annual income of fifteen thousand rupees (which we must forget about) but two checks of 583 rupees, 666 rupees and 66 paise only. More than enough to survive on, for the three of us.

Despite her grief and her strict pieties (the house resounded with "Let us pray, pour forth we beseech Thee O Lord, Thy grace into our hearts," etc.) and the tremendous fits of dejection into which she plunged, Paro coped with everything, always raising her heavy eyelids just in time. She made a bus trip to Ranchi, collected the entrance forms for Mala from Rev. Mother Xavier, and came back with a contract from a ready-made clothing shop to do all their alterations. She threw out Mr. Roy and made Mr. Mitra draw up a new inventory, which included the discovery of seventeen gold mohurs "forgotten" in a vase, and after the notary left, calmly dismissed my protests, saying, "I can do what I want with my possessions, I hope! I used to buy one mohur as a Christmas present to myself when I could afford it. I'm in my eighties, Chchanda, and if we wait till I die, the government will take it from you anyway. The other time I showed them just the securities—for expenses. I think this gold is illegal to keep for one person, but for three? And Mr. Mitra won't talk anyway. We have to make some repairs on this house: keep a good kitchen garden, Mala's expenses for her studies, and I've always wanted to keep two cows and two men to help out."

Generosity of this kind makes its own fetters and gratitude merely turns the key in the lock. Paro was rewarding me for my repentance, imposing a confidence that would be impossible to betray. What would I do, my God, what would I do if everything were open to question again?

And Pratap continued to prowl around our house.

Misses Elke and Eba dropped in one morning. With their usual forthrightness they said that, since Pratap seemed so keen on marrying me (everyone knew that), they felt sure Thakur Sahib wouldn't stand in the way. After all, there was precious little he could do even the last time. People have short memories, etc.

One night I heard someone whistle under my window. I withdrew into the patchwork bedcover. Paro raked over the footprints in silence next morning. She never sent me out on errands, a saunter in the woods was regarded with suspicion, and Mala or she herself was always with me.

At night whenever a horn sounded in the road, she started in her chair, although she never said a word. If you don't talk about them, your problems disappear. More often than not, the cursed horn was not the afeared one, but some wealthy farmers returning in a rented truck after a good sale in Ranchi. But once at least, I recognized the sound, as I had that time, when Pratap was our bridegroom and my aunt, the bride, failed to recognize it. I began to suffocate. It sounded in short furious blasts, like some sort of code; then longer summons, setting all the village dogs to barking, tearing at the night for miles and miles around. Without stopping my sewing, without missing a stitch, I felt the excitement growing, making every nerve alert. What did he want from me, this fainthearted lover with his nocturnal aubade interrupted with the barking of twenty dogs? Couldn't he understand? He had his chance, the chance of a wolf who gulps down the goat in three mouthfuls and who has then nothing left to do but slink off, gorged with his prey, to his old haunts, to digest his bellyful. Who wanted him to stick around here, to fasten onto his victim, like a hyena? Passions pass, and if habits endure, what right had he to consider me a habit?

But the horn blasted on louder than ever. A voice? A cry? No, just a horn. Not even the courage to come in and make a scene, not even the guts to take revenge. Instead he counted on me, on the hankering of a virginal sex urge, to take the initiative. I leapt up suddenly, my skin prickling, and sat down again. My slipper began to beat to the tune of some unknown music. "Come! Come!" said the horn working for the wolf.

Paro got up on creaking old knees. "I hate the windows to look like blind eyes," she said, and shut them.

There was a crisis every day at noon when the mail came in. Paro trembled at the very idea of watching me open a letter but I was afraid that, if I let her open them for me, she might come across some scabrous evocation of our old times together. So we watched for old Kishun, the drunken postman, together. Neither of us would have let the merest prospectus into the house without scrutinizing it carefully. You never know. And lovers have all kinds of wiles! I was even a little surprised that Pratap hadn't had recourse to some such subterfuge already. But those first days he contented himself with a single inoffensive postcard:

"There's a lot of work to do and I need you dreadfully. Come whenever you like or can. Best regards to everyone. Pratap."

Paro carefully tore the card to shreds before my eyes. It

was a picture of the Kutub Minar. Three days later, I received another one, the Taj Mahal this time:

"I can't understand why I haven't heard from you, Chchanda. You can't let yourself be shut up. You have enough spirit and more. Shall I come and see you? We have to talk. All my love, Pratap."

"Let him come," said Paro. "I have all the brooms in the house I need for him."

Pratap didn't come but a registered letter arrived, which naturally only I could receive. Paro let me take it from Kishun, but as soon as the postman's back was turned, she snatched it back from me and threw it into the kitchen fire. "All right, all right," she shouted, "since he is so fond of using postcards, which gives everyone such a good laugh, we'll use one, too!"

She rummaged out one from the confines of her room. It was a yellowed picture of Patna's Golghar. "Now write," she said, "Dear Pratap, We are through with you. Please don't bother us anymore. Your niece, Madhuchchanda."

She stood over me while I wrote. "But wouldn't silence be better, Paro?" I asked timidly.

"Silence doesn't say 'no.' "

I painfully wrote out the "Madhuchchanda." To associate my aunt's name with the dismissal she would never have signed. It was a good symbol though, striking out the past with the future. I made the mistake of turning the card over and suddenly my head seemed so heavy, so heavy and huge, just like the Golghar. "Sher Shah would have known what to do," I believe I said, and fainted at Paro's feet.

Chapter 24

Standing in front of my mirror, I took another look at myself, Chchanda, Madhuchchanda. There was no use struggling against the evidence any longer. It wasn't a coincidence; not even a matter of doubt. I really deserved the old riddle they vulgarly asked: What is the difference between a woman who has been sleeping around and a new recruit? And the answer, equally vulgar: For the first twenty-eight days, a new recruit is afraid he might have to see blood; the woman is afraid she may not. I use this dreadful little joke on purpose, its very coarseness serving to emphasize the disgust that is the first reaction of a foolish woman, who still can't believe that the same thing that happened to the servant-girls in back rooms had happened to her. Love always has its own decor, spins its own thread, even if it's a black one, and never feels the grub stirring in the web, until suddenly there's a nice, sordid, banal surprise that leaves your underwear unstained and yourself a girl no longer. I couldn't fool Parvati much more. But today is Sunday and she is at church. So let's go out, out to the Koel's edge, and think it over. Decide what I want—what I can still do. Who would hesitate in a case like mine? My champion wasn't exactly remote. A postcard and fifteen minutes with him would solve the problem. Like Madhulika's. Already.

Already! It was more a question of insurance than a consolation. I was still undecided. Dr. Bose? No, he would never agree to nor perform an abortion, especially if he knew there was a solution at hand. I'd have to think about it more clearly. Poor Madhulika. Hadn't I exulted enough that your marriage had the same excuse? Did it have to be my turn now? And in a situation that was much worse, so that I would have to say to a man I had already rejected, "No, I didn't want you anymore. But I have to become a tradition! There's always someone pregnant enough at Panditji's House to marry you. This time, at least, get a doctor's certificate!"

Despised by the father, imposing on the son, what else could happen except perhaps to have my husband forget, as the last straw, how he became my lover in the first place? Whatever they say, a man who gets a wife with a full belly eventually remembers it. And, after all, what separated me from Pratap yesterday held good today too, and would keep us apart forever. If the consequences of a mistake could cancel it out, or in another form, actually make it creditable, agreeable to man, God, and the law alike, it would all be much too easy. Once the punishment was chosen, it carried itself out automatically, regardless of redeeming factors, overwhelming half of Chchanda, without touching the other. This child was mine and mine alone.

To establish a connection with Pratap half as strong as the cord that bound it to me, to be called "Singh," that name would have to be spoken at Panditji's House for the first time, so that I wouldn't feel I was creating life by robbing death, I would have to . . . I was raving, of course, but the house itself, decked out with all its wild flowers, seemed to follow my thoughts—as if the wild roses didn't know how to finish the work by themselves! As if the pollen hadn't done enough! As if, a child, once conceived, couldn't be born without a father! He had done his work, hadn't he? The rest was up to me!

A crane suddenly clapped his wings together and screeched his approval, flying towards Thakur Sahib's estate. I sat down on the bank, mechanically untying my sandals in my old way, letting the water gush between my toes. Smooth and slow, the currents spun the reeds into long, greenish, white thread. I could see clearly the trap that one of Thakur Sahib's minions had laid out and felt the urge to steal once again. It would have been more appropriate to have thought about playing Ophelia among those long reeds that look so becoming in the hair of drowned girls. The Koel flows down into Ranchi, and maybe Pratap would be out walking and see me float by. . . .

Anyway, that's what Paro must have thought I was thinking. The twigs suddenly snapped behind me and she appeared, pretending to be gathering wood. The way she walked, the way she held her head, the way she was breathing—everything told me a scene was about to be held. Can one blame her?

"You don't know what day of the month it is? You have to put your feet in the water and catch something too?" But that was only the prologue to force me out of my silence, and putting on my sandals wouldn't do me a bit of good. "Dear Virgin Mary," she groaned, "that's all we needed!" Then her anger got the best of her and she began screaming, "Go on, tell me it isn't true, tell me. Just try to deny it, you little animal! What you've got under your skin to make you go down on your back—and with whom—and at what a time! And then you sit there dreaming! What an example for Mala, and what a life ahead for you! They're going to think well of me around here! How well I've brought you up! I'm glad Madhu isn't around to see this. . . ."

Suddenly she wasn't angry anymore. I wasn't alone and my guilt was somehow protected by the innocence within me. My friend and ally, the Koel, told her nothing of my thoughts. "Come with me," she said roughly, "I want to talk to you. I mean, I'll talk. Closemouthed as you are, where will I get my answers?"

Paro slowly panted up the slope. I was reminded of the day, just a few months ago, when I stole Uncle Katla and Aunt Rui. Was I still the same girl? I couldn't have said it aloud, but Paro said, "Well, you are what you are. I can't make you change anything." She was suffering deeply and my heart was wrung dry for her. "You can have Pratap any day, I suppose. Even Thakur Sahib will consent with an heir on the way, and you, a young, lovely, healthy girl. The properties can be joined. Madhu was not exactly the daughter-in-law of his dreams. But Chchanda, will it last? What is it based on?" She did not ask for a single detail; she never would.

Behind her the frangipani tree bared its nicks and notches. Paro must have shrunk these past years, for we had made her mark too, one day, all of us screaming with laughter. And now, her topknot passed easily under the notch in the bark. She grinned weakly, "It's all right for him—a fine part to play. He holds on to his girl, he warms his blood, and you get your aunt's leavings. In ten years you'll have your man grumbling about his arthritis and you'll be in full bloom. I tell you, Chchanda, you can love somebody up here [pointing to her head] or down there [pointing elsewhere], and I don't think you've tried it up here yet. I've known about it for a long time. If you really wanted to, you could have gone with him. But you didn't. You were guilty about it and Panditji's House held you. You told yourself it wouldn't be such a good idea to try on your aunt's wedding ring while it was still warm from her *chita*. The dead can take care of themselves better than the living. What you have against them vanishes like breath; what you've done to them nails you to the cross."

Silence, a long silence except the continuous call of a cicada. "It's all true," said Paro, "when you've done something like that together, and I don't mean the act of sex, but the terrible betrayal, each of you ends up blaming the other. Pratap will think to himself, How could she do that to her own aunt who was dying? And to spare himself, he'll decide you threw yourself at him. And you, Chchanda, will start to think, he violated you, spoiled you; you'll get to hate a man capable of that and capable of switching from aunt to niece. A mended plate always breaks in the same place. Chchanda, it's not my place to give you advice about these things. There are other things to consider, the name of the father, his family, his money—it all means something. I could go and see Pratap if you like."

"No, Paro. I am not going to marry him." The words fell of their own accord from my lips. Paro shuddered and stepped away from me, as if she felt guilty of her own arguments or my decision.

A sudden suspicion brought her close to me again. "You aren't going to try to harm the baby, are you?"

"No, Paro. Never."

Her wrinkles slackened. Her voice became almost warm. "If you make the best of it, a baby grows up after all. And you know where to send back the stones they will throw at you. And it will have the very best of grandmothers, Chchanda."

Now, if only she wouldn't take out her checked handkerchief! She began sniffling and coughing, but still had enough of her peasant's tact and wit to know how to unstring the trembles when they started getting embarrassing. She quickly began again in her usual bittersweet voice, "And this time, I promise you, I'll keep an eye on you. You will eat the best of everything. . . ."

But of course, Paro, whatever you say. It's over now, our words have all been spoken. If you've guessed everything, there isn't much you can hide, either. I know what you are hoping for, and what a price I'll have to pay for the sour isolation in which our old prickly friendship will revive. The dishonoring of a girl, to whom you have been more a mother than anyone else, no matter how long you hide it, will have to come out in the long run, and the gossip of the whole village at your heels is not an easy thing to bear. It doesn't do much good to toss your head like that, even though it is at the thought of a child that will keep away suitors for good and all: a child who will make them leave us as we are, by ourselves, at Panditji's House. Paro, you who are so unafraid, why does change frighten you so much?

Chapter 25

To tell the truth, I was really hoping for a daughter and so was Paro, who began sewing all kinds of things in pink and white. I even knew her name, which mustn't be spoken ahead of time, though every tree-trunk at Panditji's house already bore its capital *M*.

Almost two months had gone since Pratap was last here. The weather began to grow mellow and the sunshine translucent. Great silences pressed upon the noon in the living room of Panditji's House where the hum of the Singer machine was constant. Bright scraps of cloth and thread were everywhere. From time to time Paro stretched out an arm for a button or a ribbon, dryly broke off the end of a thread on one of her strong old teeth, glanced over at me with an eye as sharp as her needle, then immediately leaned over her work again. Neither smiling nor sulking, her face expressed a twofold reserve: partly the result of grief and partly what indulgence granted. She had nothing to say except our daily banalities. Nothing to spy on except a few inoffensive gestures—the way my foot swung back and forth under the table; the way my arm twisted behind me to open the catch of a brassière that had grown a little too tight; and soon after, the way my body started with surprise at a sudden movement within it, as if uncertain whether to be offended or to try to control the signal by pressing a hand over my swollen bulk.

Warped by so many pressures, painful from so many sores, our old friendship had never quite returned, of course: we needed much more time, more resignation, more forgetfulness. There was still one threat: the reaction of Thakur Sahib across the river if my secret ever travelled there. But we were together, we attended to our shame. Mala studied in earnest towards the scholarship from St. Xavier's—all in a house that had been saved, in a lost sweetness, where my absent aunt finally recovered her advantage over my missing lover, and where what was no more finally triumphed over what would never be.

And the time concerned itself only with passing. It was remarkable how the meaning of a life could fill so few days, and then become months and months before you encountered a date that signified anything, arising from the slow current of habits. We built a cow-shed with the help of two village idiots. Once upon a time we used to have a man who "did" for us. He quit when Pratap had asked him to shine his car for him. We built a hen-coop and bought fifteen Rhode Island birds. And finally two pregnant cows. Like them, I felt enormous: the unexpected startles you and a pregnant girl always seems larger than a married one in the same condition.

It was scarcely possible to hide any longer. We had held out until the last possible minute, refusing to let anyone know—not only the interested parties but even the doctor whose attentions my almost insolent health permitted me to postpone. Nevertheless, the news spread far and wide.

In our part of the country, the worst misconduct is half exonerated if it can imitate the hollow tree that keeps its fine bark on the surface and rots away at the heart. But an unmarried mother, exposing her belly and her example, has really fallen. And that, too, Panditji's granddaughter. I felt a sort of painful satisfaction at withstanding the glances fixed on my girth: when someone else despises you, you don't have to despise yourself, and the wound you were keeping open cauterizes itself with a scorn other than your own.

I didn't know what to do with myself those last days. I distrusted my own thoughts, which, too often for comfort, in spite of my postcard, wondered at the sudden silence. At least the gossip of the village ought to have caused some reaction! I began to read whatever I could find in the house, old Bengali classics of my grandfather's, his store of English books, and recent ones that Madhulika had devoured on her sickbed. These last were all about love and purity or about adultery and socialism. Everybody in them had one thing in common—personal uncleanliness. Everyone slept around with no care in the world except not to have a child—the last remaining definitive proof of their feminity. I could not identify with my ancestors—either they were too worthy or not at all. Surely Devdas could have taken a stand? And I couldn't identify with my contemporaries either, despite their Amazonian liberty. Or because of it. I was from Panditji's House where no one's good example could be followed any more than one could be set.

My book would fall from my hands, and sometimes I would write out (in my head of course) a scene worthy of myself, imagining Pratap's sudden return some Sunday (Paro would be at church) to come and carry me off. I would have turned the key in the lock so as not to be taken by surprise. He wouldn't get near me, thanks to my discretion. I would play deaf. Or better still, I would open the window first, so that he could see only my head and shoulders and not guess what had happened below. From my high perch, I would be in a good spot to take my turn at screaming, "Get out of here!" and if he shouted, "It will be *my* child too!" I would answer, "Surely, Mr. Singh, you're enough of a jurist to know that *pater is est quem nuptiae demonstrat:* in adultery, paternity is . . ."

And then, if he insisted, I would insist right back, holding on to the window sill, so as not to give an inch, "Look here, Pratap, if I didn't tell you about the baby, I had my reasons. You don't owe me anything." And he would go away stunned with grief, and drink himself to death, like Devdas, who couldn't take a stand, either.

I suppose I'll always have that scene on my conscience.

Our imagination is always a flatterer and the truth was much simpler. Wagner had somehow heard about it and his son's humiliation and sent him off to Calcutta. Paro had known all about it and chose to tell me thus:

Miss Elke: "How is Chchanda keeping, Paro?"

Paro: "Very well. Have you heard that that Anglo-Indian girl who got pregnant is getting married? Her rascal has returned from the city he got away to and has decided to make an honest woman of her."

Miss Elke: Dead silence.

Paro: "Our rascal has gone to Calcutta. The atmosphere around here is too cold for him. Ha!"

Better informed than others, Miss Elke didn't entirely credit the official version that was doing the rounds these days, in which Pratap was depicted as a real cad, "attacking a mere child like that? He should be lynched!"

She was a trifle surprised at my resignation and carelessness at losing even a cad like that. "Don't worry, Chchanda. It can still be arranged. If it's a boy, you will most certainly hear from Thakur Sahib. . . ." My black scowl cut her off.

Next day, on the first of January, my daughter Madhumita was born.

Chapter 26

Broken, bitter weather, grey and undecided. The river was still low this year. "Too cold for Madhumita," said my sister Mala. She was holding my baby like a Ming vase. But it wasn't too cold or too hot for my daughter, wrapped as she was with only the tip of her nose showing. I had inoculated her with my blood and my breast—the Netarhat cold was never going to affect her. Besides, an inadequate sun was coming out. My eyes closed. It must have been . . . But I didn't keep track anymore except in relation to the baby . . . Let's see, it must have been two months ago that she started walking, five months ago that she sat up by herself, ten since she was born, nine and ten since she was conceived, twenty-five months since her father brought my aunt back as a bride, changing sides of the Koel to live with us.

What if he came again? Came and said, "Chchanda, I understand you now. I didn't mean anything to you. I'll come; I'll go away again. I'll leave you alone at Panditji's

House. But once in a while, out here, on the bank of the river . . ." Luckily there isn't much chance of finding a man willing to appear at a nymph's merest sigh. Or to vanish at her frown.

Each to her post. Madhumita in her pen. Paro at her machine, Mala at her Junior College. The wind is rising outside. Paro gets up to shut the windows and put a little oil in the Singer. Yes, first we need a little oil to let the rest flow smoothly. "By the way, Chchanda, Thakur Sahib has had a heart attack. He is very bad. They say that Pratap will come back." And her eyes grow troubled as they had not been for months, confessing what she dared not add, If he comes back to attack, shall my old arms have to take up weapons again?

No, Paro, no. Even that thought is unfair. There are things you don't know. Thakur Sahib has met me twice, sauntering in the woods; the first time with my swollen belly. "Why will you not marry Pratap?" he has asked.

And honestly, I have answered, "I cannot let him intrude."

I am not afraid of Pratap anymore. The argument he would find readiest to his tongue would be just the one to condemn him most surely. Already conquered by Panditji's House, how could he overcome it now, in the name of the daughter of the house who had become its very future?

If I hadn't known it before, I knew it now. I knew enough not to mention that second meeting with Thakur Sahib on the banks of the Koel, with Madhumita in my arms. "Why do you girls call me Wagner? Am I so loud?" I don't answer, but I smile. "Chchanda," he says, "when you have vast acres to shout across, you have to shout loud. May yours increase and multiply. You understood the land. Panditji had his convert's zeal; but he should never have left Calcutta and academics. Your mother hated it here. Your aunt had very little choice. And Pratap . . . Pratap does not feel for the soil as you and I do. Maybe, Madhumita . . . but I will long be dead by then."

Now I say to Paro, "Why don't you leave those people alone? We have nothing to do with them."

Paro lights up like a candle. It is the same smile that had drawn aside her wrinkles the day Dr. Bose asked for a towel and let her dry my baby.

Let her scold me in her fits of rage, let her be as thorny as our hedges, determined, like them, to surround me on all sides. It doesn't matter at all. That she knows my faults is all right, too; I know her weaknesses. If we had to be proud of the people we loved, whom would we love?

Enough of these complications. Better to finish these French knots for that trousseau for that female's wedding next month; it is an order from those rich people in town.

I bathe and put Madhumita to bed. Then I go down. Under my feet, the sixth stair never creaks, and when I open the front door, the hinges are silent. How calm it is, Chchanda! The trees have left off their moaning; the wind has only served to sweep the sky clear. A tree-toad hovers tirelessly between its two notes, suddenly striking the pitch in between just as a star falls. And the light and the song continue, fade, and die away together. How well I understand that. But tenderness betrayed, guilty love, will you never forgive me, Madhulika? Was I born for this, whatever you have left me? I ask for no more and I forget nothing, alas. And I take care of myself, just as Panditji's House takes care of itself—as much devoured as defended by its briars and its memories.

So once more, the inventory: Here I am with a family, a property, and therefore an address, of certain reputation, a little accomplishment, a few worries, a regret here and there, and many memories, some to be cherished, most to be expunged—and soonest.

INDRANI AIKATH-GYALTSEN was born in Chaibasa, Bihar, in 1952. She went to school in Jamshedpur and later moved to New York City where she studied at Barnard College. She lives at present in Darjeeling, where, in addition to being a free-lance journalist, she owns and runs a hotel. She is married to a tea planter, and has one son.